# LEGENDS OF THE

# DRAGON

# COWBOYS

**The Venerable Travels of Ling Fung
by David B. Riley
&
Chin Song Ping and the Long, Long Night
by Laura Givens**

# LEGENDS OF THE
# DRAGON
# COWBOYS

**The Venerable Travels of Ling Fung
by David B. Riley
&
Chin Song Ping and the Long, Long Night
by Laura Givens**

Hadrosaur Productions, Mesilla Park, NM

Legends of the Dragon Cowboys
First Edition, first printing, continuous printing on demand
First date of publication: October 2017
Editor: David Lee Summers
Cover Art: Laura Givens

ISBN: 1-885093-83-7

Hadrosaur Productions
P.O. Box 2194
Mesilla Park, NM 88047-2194
www.hadrosaur.com

Published by Hadrosaur Productions

# TABLE OF CONTENTS

# LEGENDS OF THE
# DRAGON
# COWBOYS

# INTRODUCTION
David Lee Summers

Chinese Immigration to America boomed around 1850, soon after the end of the First Opium War and during the period of the California Gold Rush. Chinese men came to America to search for gold, work on the transcontinental railroads, and work on Southern Plantations after the American Civil War. American businessmen welcomed this source of cheap labor, but many American workers feared the Chinese immigrants.

Only merchants were allowed to bring wives across, but most Chinese men who came to America planned to stay just a short time and return home. All too often, these men found themselves so deeply in debt that they couldn't return home. What's more, unlike their European counterparts, Chinese immigrants were barred from citizenship. Only the children of Chinese immigrants were allowed to become citizens.

The stories in this volume are set during this period of rapid change filled with both opportunity and strife. Cultures clashed, new marvels were invented, and often times magic and myths took on a life of their own. I've had the fortune of publishing stories by David B. Riley and Laura Givens in my magazines *Hadrosaur Tales* and *Tales of the Talisman*. They know their history and they know how to spin a good tale.

David B. Riley's Ling Fung is a merchant who only wants to open a gun store in California. Not only does he have to deal with his family, he has to contend with a Mayan god, outlaws, and even the abominable snowman. Laura Givens' Chin Song Ping comes to America seeking his fortune, but runs afoul of everything from Native American spirits to Voodoo despots.

Turn the page and learn how these "Dragon Cowboys" adapt to life in the strange frontier known as the American West.

# THE VENERABLE TRAVELS OF LING FUNG

David B. Riley

# 1
## ASSASSIN

Ling Fung sipped his tea. Tea in America just wasn't the same as tea in China, but at least it was something hot. He didn't think he would ever get warm again. This godforsaken town was so incredibly cold. Ah, the steaming hot cup of tea was his only refuge. Of course, he could work downstairs in his brother's laundry business. It was plenty warm down there. He sighed. How he missed his home in China. If only the Emperor had not ordered him killed. "What is it, Lotus Blossom?"

"Why do you call me that?"

The insolent child. America was corrupting the youth. "You remind me of someone."

"There's some white guy to see you," she said.

Some white guy? That was odd. Where had that insolent child gone off to? He made his way down the stairs and opened the door. There was indeed some white guy standing there on the porch. "The laundry is around on the other side of the building."

"Are you Ling Fung? That girl said you were home."

"How may I be of service to you?" He gestured for the man to come inside. That way he could get the door closed and try and keep warm.

"Name's Rusty Calhoun. I run a mining operation just out of town, here." He took off his tan Stetson. They must've called him Rusty on account of his red hair. "Big Ponderosa Mine, it's a small placer gold operation."

"Again, how may I be of service to you?"

"Well, I don't know much about these things. I guess I'll just be to the point. I need to have somebody killed."

"I see. Would you like some tea?"

"Thank you, no."

"Well, I do not believe I can help you. We Chinese do not all belong to violent tongs."

"I don't know what a tong is, frankly."

"Well, then why do you think I would even be interested in killing someone for you?"

"These are all over town." He reached into his pocket and produced a flyer, which he unfolded.

Need someone killed?
Famous Chinese Assassin Ling Fung now in America
Contact at 22 ½ Main Street
Affordable rates.

"Lotus Blossom!"

"What is it now?" the insolent child asked.

"Do you know anything about these flyers?"

"Father says the only way to get you to move out is if you find work and you're only good for killing people. So, I made some flyers for you to drum up some business."

This conversation was getting most unusual. "Mr. Calhoun, are you sure you would not like some tea? Ah, even better, would you like to sample some Chinese beer?"

Rusty's face lit up. "Chinese make beer?"

"Yes. We invented it." At least, that was what he was always told growing up. Uncle Ho was brew master at the brewery back in China. Some bottles of beer had just arrived, in fact. Uncle Ho was a wonderful man, sending beer all the way from Qingdao by clipper ship. He clapped his hands. "Lotus Blossom, bring us some beer."

"Stop calling me that," the insolent child replied. But she did bring two bottles of beer. And she even remembered the glasses to drink it out of. Drinking straight from the bottle was uncivilized.

After gulping down about half the glass, Rusty announced, "This stuff is pretty good."

"It is not easy to come by. My uncle manages to send me some now and then. Now then, why would you need to obtain my services?"

"Well, sir, it's kind of hard to explain, but I'll try."

Ling Fung clapped his hands. "Another beer?"

"Sure, that's good beer. Well sir, I hired some coolie, er

Chinese workers for my mine. Good boys, damn good workers. We were looking for a new vein of ore, then this guy come along and took all my workers. Mining's what you call a labor intensive business. Well, I tracked down this guy. He's got a mine of his own up on the Nevada border. And somehow he's hypnotized everyone to work for him. I don't think he even pays them."

"I see. And you want me to go and kill this man?"

"Well sir, he also took $20,000 in gold from me. You can keep that for your fee. Just get my miners back. And, that feller, well I figure you'll have to kill him to accomplish that. Damn, this is good beer."

"And, who is this feller?"

"Calls himself Ah Puch."

"That is a most unusual name. It does not sound American or Chinese."

Rusty nodded. "Oh, he ain't from around here. He's from down Mexico way, Yucatan Peninsula they call it."

"Very well. I will take care of your problem for you."

"Outstanding." Rusty finished his beer and put his Stetson back on.

"What does this man look like?"

"Has the head of an owl on the body of a man."

"Excuse me?"

Rusty had only consumed two beers. He was most certainly not inebriated. "Yep, that's what he looks like. They say he's a Mayan god or something." With that, Rusty departed.

Ling Fung sank into his comfortable chair and consumed another glass of beer. What had he just gotten himself into?

He set out on his journey the next morning. And he thought Placerville was too darn cold. Wherever this godforsaken trail was taking him, this was much worse. He'd heard parts of China were this cold, but he'd always lived in the warm part. This was simply awful. Americans had an obsession with gold. But he had to admit, $20,000 was a lot of money and would improve his lifestyle considerably. So he pulled the collar of his coat tighter around his neck to delude himself that it somehow kept him warmer and trudged on into the high Sierra. Why would a Mayan god come to such a horrible place? Surely they must have gold in Mexico.

Then he remembered tales of treasure ships. The Spanish had stolen all of their gold. No wonder this Mayan god had to come to America to get more. And so he and his horse trudged on as the cold wind howled around them.

He made camp that night. The Ponderosa pines provided an abundant supply of firewood and he kind of enjoyed tossing pine cones into the flames and listening to them crackle. In spite of his fire, it was still so incredibly cold. He huddled and shivered and finally daylight came and he could resume his journey.

Finally, they arrived at a fenced-in area where there was sign above the gate that read OWL MINE. This had to be the place. A man dressed in a gray uniform of some kind sat just behind the gate. The area seemed completely surrounded by a fence.

"Excuse me," Ling Fung said.

"Get lost you damned coolie. We ain't hiring."

What a pleasant individual. "You misunderstand. I have not come seeking work. I wish to see person in charge, please."

"Screw off." The man rested his hand on a holstered revolver. Looked like a Colt Navy.

"Very well. I had wished to avoid bloodshed." He climbed down off his horse.

"It's your blood, coolie."

Ling Fung threw a shuriken. The throwing star tore into the man's arm just above the wrist. "You will find it most difficult to shoot me now."

"Damn, this hurts." He struggled to draw his gun, but couldn't as the sharp blades had severed the tendons in his arm. He tried to draw with his left hand.

Ling Fung simply climbed over the gate and took the gun away from the man. "I can kill you, if you desire to save face with your employer."

"Damned coolie. God this hurts."

Ling Fung delivered a simple blow to the man's sternum, sending him sprawling on the ground. "Business here concluded." He opened the gate and climbed back up on his horse. He should have killed him, but he felt sorry for this guy in some odd way.

He was amazed how poorly guarded this mine was. Of course, why waste workers standing around guarding the place when they can be mining ore. He rode right up to a cluster of ramshackle buildings and canvas tents. Only at that point did the many guys working on things seem to even notice him. Suddenly, there were any number of firearms pointed in his direction

"What you want here, coolie?" one of the gray-clad men inquired. "How'd you get in here?"

Ling Fung announced. "I have business with someone known as Ah Puch."

"How dare you say the name of our great lord!"

Ling Fung quietly and calmly climbed down off his horse. He approached the man doing the yelling. Then he took the man's pistol out of his hand in one sweeping move. It was a shame the Shaolin Monastery had not worked out. Ling Fung had enjoyed learning Kung Fu. A rapid blow to this man's sternum sent him to the dirt. "I am Ling Fung. I desire to see Ah Puch. Am I in the wrong place?"

"No, coolie, you ain't in the wrong place. Be careful what you wish for," another guy in gray said.

Four men in orange robes came out of one of the buildings. They motioned for him to follow. He was taken to a nearby amphitheater and told to sit on a bench in the audience section. The guys in the robes knelt at the edge of the stage. Everything was quiet for a few moments, then a procession approached. It was led by more guys in orange robes. What followed was a creature in a man's body, dressed also in a gray uniform, but it had the head of an owl. Ling Fung had dearly hoped that it would not really be an owl head, but simply a mask of some sort. That did not seem to be the case. It really did look like an owl head.

The owl man sat in an oversized chair that sort of reminded Ling Fung of the imperial throne in Peking. "Well, you came here demanding to see me. Here I am."

"You took the workers and $20,000 in gold from the Big Ponderosa Mine in Placerville. This is not acceptable. I demand their immediate return."

"Well, I can say no one has ever had the courage to come to me and make such a demand. Of course, it may not be courage but mere stupidity." He had a high, squeaky voice. Of course owls don't usually talk. He stood. "I am Ah Puch. I am a Mayan god. I have come to California to make it my own country, devoted solely to serve me. No other need is of any concern." He sat back down in his big chair. "The choice is yours. You can work in the mine or you can die."

"I gave you an opportunity to resolve this matter. It is unfortunate you have chosen not to."

"Do you really think you are going to kill me? Do you not know Ah Puch cannot be killed?" He pointed to some of the gray-clad men. "But I am quite sure you can be killed."

"Most unfortunate." Ling Fung stood from his bench and pulled the nunchakus from his coat. "Most unfortunate." It was in situations like this that he wished he had a Japanese katana sword used by the Samurai. But his immediate concern was the man with the rifle. He swung the nunchakus, knocking the closest adversary unconscious. Ling Fung then grabbed the body just as the rifleman fired. The body absorbed the bullet. He then threw one of his few remaining shurikens, which landed in the rifleman's neck.

It was time to thin out this crowd. He grabbed the rifle from the man he'd just killed and emptied the chamber. How nice these repeating Winchesters were, compared to the old single-shot rifles. He might just keep this one. When he was out of bullets, he reclaimed the shuriken and spun and threw it at Ah Puch, who was still standing on the stage watching the fight. A well placed kick, then a blow to the head eliminated the last of the nearby gray-clad men.

Ah Puch seemed amused with the Chinese throwing star embedded in his chest. He reached down and removed it by simply yanking it out. He held it up and examined it. "I have heard of these, but never actually seen one. A most impressive weapon. I'll have to get me some." With astonishing speed, he threw the shuriken directly at Ling Fung.

The nunchakus deflected the throwing star, sending it harmlessly into the dirt. Ling Fung went over and picked it up. Even though the few remaining of Ah Puch's men had fled, he had few weapons left and certainly did not want somebody else to pick it up and try and use it or give it back to the bird man.

"And, you probably think I am bleeding to death from my wounds. I was not joking or bragging when I said Ah Puch cannot be killed. I am the Mayan god of death. I know well what it takes to kill an adversary. And this is not it, though I do commend you for your fighting skills. I was most impressed." With that, the owl part of him separated from the man part. A full-sized owl flew away from the neck cavity of a very dead body that immediately dropped to the floor of the stage. The owl flew straight at Ling Fung, who readied his nunchakus, then seemed to think better of it and flew off in the direction of the mine entrance.

A few moments later, Ah Puch emerged from the mine entrance with a new human body. It was apparently one of his own guards and not a miner, as it was clad in one of the gray uniforms.

"Just remember, when you are traveling, owls hunt at night," Ah Puch yelled. Then he climbed up on a horse and rode away.

It took a moment to sink in that the only horse around was his own. The bird man had just stolen his horse. Ling Fung approached the mine.

The Chinese workers were wandering out. They all seemed in a daze. "Venerable," and that was a term he was not used to being called, one of the miners asked, "Where are we? This is not the Big Ponderosa Mine. How did we get here?"

"An evil spell has been placed over you. Gather everyone around and I will explain. Then we will take you all back to Placerville." Ah Puch might have lost his horse and saddle, but he was going to keep the Winchester. And, although the Chinese miners were most grateful at being freed by him, Ling Fung never found the $20,000 in gold.

# 2
## BOUNTY HUNTERS

Ling Fung tossed another stick on the fire. There just didn't seem to be any warmth coming from the flames. "Why is this place so blasted cold? I haven't been warm since we left Guangdong."

The brown dog just stared blankly at him. Dog had never been to Guangdong.

"You're not even cold. Why don't you ever get cold? They say Arizona is hot. Why isn't it hot?" He tossed another stick on the fire. He'd made his fire low, in a dugout pit like Uncle Ho had taught him. "Build a small fire and sit up close so no one can see your fire. Build a big fire and sit up close. That's what I think. Why are we in this horrible place? I'll never be warm again?"

Dog started growling.

"Relax. That's just some man crawling around in the bushes. It's not a squirrel."

The dog continued growling.

"Go to Arizona, brother say." He tried again to warm his hands. "So I end up on the side of this mountain, freezing." Dog was not much good for conversation. Neither was the man hiding in the bushes. The dog continued growling.

"Now we sit on Mt. Lemmon in the cold. At least in California we had tea." A cup of tea would be so warming. The dog did not seem to care. Ling Fung picked up a rock and hurled it into the darkness.

"Ow."

"You are making my dog upset. Why don't you come out of the bushes?"

A white man emerged from the shadows. He had a Winchester repeater trained on them. "Don't move coolie."

"You have been watching me for half an hour and I have not moved. Why would I be likely to move now?" Ling Fung asked.

"I been looking fer you fer a long time, coolie."

"Why would anyone be looking for me?" The sad reality was, although the Emperor had ordered his execution, China didn't really want him back. They told Uncle Ho, "America could have him," when they learned of Ling Fung's departure from Shanghai.

The man unrolled a parchment. "Yep, finally got you." The parchment listed a bandit known as Way Fong, described as six feet tall and a powerful build. "A thousand dollars bounty."

"You are a bounty hunter, then?"

"And you're wanted dead or alive."

"By the Mexican government no less. I did not think they liked giving out rewards to gringos."

"They want you bad."

"Not all that bad. That is for a thousand pesos, not American dollars. You will be very disappointed at the exchange rate." Ling Fung slowly stood. "Two things: First, I am only five foot eight inches tall. Second, I have never visited the fine country of Mexico."

"You Chinee all look alike."

"So I keep hearing. I wish I could persuade you to move on."

"Not hardly likely."

"I am not the coolie you are looking for. Now move on or I will be forced to use violence."

"I got the rifle, coolie."

With a graceful motion the shuriken throwing star flew from Ling Fung's hand, across the camp, and into the throat of the bounty hunter. The bounty hunter promptly fell to the ground, unable to breathe and blood spurted from his neck.

Ling Fung picked up the Winchester rifle. "How many of these do we have now?"

The dog did not answer.

"I would think at least ten of them back in Placerville, assuming brother has not sold them. What are we going to do with all these rifles? Back in Guangdong I could be a warlord with so many rifles." He looked down at the bounty hunter. "So sorry, I thought you were dead. Rude to take things until after you are gone. Will wait."

When the bounty hunter finally stopped twitching, Ling Fung placed the rifle in his saddle bags. He looked over the wanted poster for a moment then tossed the poster in the fire. He still had four hours of shivering until morning. He dragged the body over to the edge of the nearby cliff and tossed it over. "Buzzards take care of the rest." He returned to the fire.

"Come dog," he ordered as the first rays of dawn sliced through the forest. "We go to desert now. Get warm."

"Not so fast, coolie," a voice ordered from behind a tree. A man emerged. He had a rifle pointed at Ling Fung. It was another Winchester.

"I sure wish I could get a Sharps rifle or even a Remington. All they ever have is Winchesters."

"Who you talkin' to, coolie?"

"The dog likes to be kept informed."

The man had a badge of some kind pinned on his buckskin vest. "I got a wagon parked down below."

"May I ask what you are arresting me for?"

"I'm Todd Watson, with the Texas Rangers."

"I hate to inform you, but Texas is some considerable distance away. Perhaps you should consider purchasing a map."

"Dang nabbit, I know where Texas is. I don't know where Way Fong is. Some bounty hunter was going to find him for me."

"Contrary to popular perception, we Chinese do not all know each other."

"Look, I know I'm not in blasted Texas. Way Fong done run off with my mail order bride. And, somehow, you're caught up in all this."

"Todd Watson, how do you think I am involved?"

"Because your brother arranged for May Li to come to America and marry me. I wired him in California and he sent me back a telegram that says you will find her."

"Brother seems to have omitted a few details when he sent me to Arizona. Let me get horse."

"So you can run off?"

"So we can get brother's business dealings straightened out." As if that was really possible. "We will find this Way Fong."

Todd Watson lowered his rifle. "Okay, but don't try nothing."

"Come along dog."

"What's your dog's name?" Ranger Watson asked.

"I do not know."

"You don't know your dog's name?"

"He has never told me his name." Ling Fung pointed out a gruesome sight. "That is most unsettling." There was half a gray horse lying next to the trail in a pool of blood—the back half. There were large tooth marks along the edge of the flesh.

"That your horse?"

"No. I believe it belonged to the bounty hunter." Ling Fung's brown gelding turned up right where he'd left it—fully intact.

"Bear?" Ranger Watson pointed to where he'd left his horse, which was also still in one piece.

"Perhaps, but it would be an unusually powerful one to take a hunk like that and devour half a horse. There is no blood trail. It was consumed here."

"I'm thinking we should head for Tombstone, that's a mining town around thirty mile or so. Guy we're looking for has worked as a miner from what I hear. That's the closest mining town."

They rode a few miles. As they descended to a lower elevation, it gradually grew a little warmer. "Curious thing about the wanted poster the bounty hunter carried?"

"What's that?" Ranger Watson asked.

"Did not say what Way Fong's crime in Mexico was."

"Oh, he ran off with May Li. The Governor of the Chihuahua was planning on marrying her."

He was speechless. Ling Fung decided to remain so. Further comment questioning the point of chasing after some woman wanted by at least three men, well it could come to nothing positive. He wondered if his brother had sold her to all three men.

"I been meaning to ask you, what were you doing on Mt. Lemmon?"

"Shivering." Ling Fung thought for a moment. "Brother said I was to meet someone there. He never showed up."

"Your brother's got some explaining to do."

It was approaching dusk when they rode into town. Tombstone was a ramshackle assortment of permanent buildings and canvas tents.

"Let's grab a drink at the saloon. See if anyone's seen this Way Fong, or my betrothed for that matter." As they entered the Oriental Saloon and Gambling Parlor, the ground shook violently beneath their feet. "Earthquake?" Ranger Watson asked, having never before actually experiencing one.

"No, that's just the men blasting under the town," one of the saloon girls said. "You'll get used to it."

"Couple beers," Ranger Watson ordered. They took a couple of seats at an empty table near a faro game that was going on.

Turned out no one had any idea who Way Fong was, or admitted to having seen May Li. They rented a room, parked their horses at the town's livery, and decided to call it a night.

At first Todd Watson thought Ling Fung snored rather loudly for a man of modest size. Then it started occurring to him it wasn't his roommate making the horrendous racket. He turned the oil lamp up from a gentle glow so he could actually see something. The dog was on his back, snoring away.

"Dog snores some," Ling Fung said. "Takes getting used to."

"Good lord, I never heard anything like that."

"More concerned with man lurking outside window."

Todd Watson grabbed his Winchester and opened the window. "Get in here!"

A man entered the room. The ranger patted him down, but found no weapons. "Why are you outside? I said we'd settle this honorably."

"I was supposed to meet Ling Ming's brother near prospector's cabin. He never showed up," the man explained in a thick Mexican accent. He was about forty, somewhat short, with a stocky build and a bald head which contrasted with a thick bushy mustache.

"That's his brother, here."

"There is no prospector's cabin," Ling Fung explained.

"Yeah, I kind of figured that out. I am Carlos de Bourbon,

Governor of Chihuahua, Mexico."

"That your wanted poster put out from Mexico?" Ling Fung asked.

"Yes, it is. I awaited the arrival of my May Li at the train station. She no more than stepped foot off the train and this brute grabbed here over his shoulder and whisked her away. I have been looking for her ever since."

"Can't the three of you find your own wives?" Ling Fung asked.

"The women in Mexico do not like me."

"The ladies in Texas just don't think I'm worth marryin'."

"My brother runs a laundry in California. He is hardly a matchmaker."

"Ad in the *Epitaph* say: 'American women hate your guts? Chinese brides want to meet you. Wire Ling Ming in Placerville, California. New railroads mean we can deliver anywhere."

"And how did you lose out on May Li?" Ling Fung asked his new roommate from Texas.

"She was supposed to be on that same train. Railroad does not go to El Paso yet, so I came over to Arizona. She got off the train. This fellow picks her up, then gets on a horse and rides off with her." He pointed at Carlos. "Then my friend here starts having some soldiers start shooting and my horse runs off, so I couldn't chase them and she was gone."

"I propose we try and get some sleep. In morning we will try and find this Way Fong."

"All right by me, but," he pointed at the dog, "I have never heard anything like that,"

Carlos de Bourbon said. "I could hear him snoring out in the street."

"Brff." the dog said as his sleep was suddenly interrupted. He made quite a splash when he hit the horse trough outside. The window was quickly closed so he couldn't get back in.

The next morning found them at the Union Café. Ranger Watson jumped out of his seat once while eating oatmeal, as the blasting underneath the town was proving tough to get used to.

The dog eyed them suspiciously when they came out of the café. After a few slices of ham, all was apparently forgiven.

"All the way from Texas? What's Way Fong done now?" the mining company foreman asked.

"I cannot really say," Ranger Watson replied. "But I do need to talk to him."

The foreman looked at Ling Fung. "Good you brought your own coolie translator 'cause he sure don't speak much English." He fumbled around with a few clipboards, took a puff off a rotgut cigar, than announced, "He didn't make his shift last night. Or the night before. If you see him, tell him he's fired."

"Know where he lives?"

"Nope."

After they were back outside, Carlos de Bourbon said, "He was a lot of help."

"Let me go on ahead," Ling Fung suggested. "I'll ask around. He's got to be staying somewhere, most likely the Chinese camp." The reality was there only a handful of Chinese people living in Tombstone at the time. It was not too much of a surprise he found Way Fong at the first tent cabin he checked.

What he found, however, was a surprise. Way Fong was sitting on the floor in the corner, wearing only a faded pink Acme Union Suit. He only vaguely acted like he was even aware of Ling Fung's presence.

"Where is May Li?"

Way Fong only said one word. Then he curled up in a ball and went to sleep.

"Gentlemen, I believe I have figured out the answers to some of your questions. Let us get underway in the wagon and I will explain on the way," Ling Fung declared.

"Where are we going?" Carlos de Bourbon asked.

"Back to Mt. Lemmon."

As they headed out of town, Ling Fung went through his saddlebags. He removed a revolver, a holster and six .36 caliber bullets. "Took Colt Navy revolver away from railroad man. Do not think he was ever in Navy."

"An accurate weapon carried by many of my colleagues with the rangers."

Ling Fung checked the Winchester taken from the bounty hunter to make sure it was loaded as well.

"Are we going to war?" Carlos de Bourbon asked.

"War may be coming to us," Ling Fung replied.

"How so?"

"Let me explain. Way Fong not in good shape."

"He was there?"

"Yes. My brother is a crook. I believe he wanted Way Fong to run off with May Li and would claim she was delivered and he would keep the money from both of you. But something else has happened, something very strange. There are tales of a hairy man beast, huge, seven feet tall—perhaps more. They inhabit forests in Russia, and even remote parts of China. It has many names. The British explorers call it Abominable Snowman, presumably as they have long white hair or fur on their bodies. The people of Tibet and western China call it Yeti."

"Sounds kind of like what the Indians call Sasquatch," Ranger Watson said. "Another ranger had a case where a farmer's daughter was carried off by one of these creatures. Never found her. Bizarre story."

"There are similarities. There are also important differences. Sasquatch is big man beast. Chinese laborers in Sierra Mountains saw them when building railroad. Sasquatch usually timid. Hides behind trees—avoids being seen. Not so, Yeti. There are certain forests in Asia the locals do not go. You go in there you not come back."

"What has this Yeti got to do with my bride?" the governor asked.

"I'm coming to that. Do not know if Way Fong mistook Sasquatch for a Yeti. He thinks Yeti took May Li. And I think Yeti is somewhere back on Mt. Lemmon."

"The horse?" Ranger Watson turned toward the governor. "Something ate half a horse like it was a sandwich."

"Exactly. I was sent there by brother. Prospector's cabin I could not find burned to ground in forest fire, according to man at newspaper office."

"If there's a prospector's cabin," the Texas Ranger reasoned, "there may be a mine tunnel of some kind."

"Exactly."

"That Colt revolver won't be much use against something that big."

"We may have to kill ourselves."

"Brff."

"Care to elaborate on that?"

"Some years ago Uncle Ho contacted me to go with him into western China, near the border with Tibet. Chinese Emperor asked him as favor. Apparently British college students went missing. They were en route to Tibet to see Dalai Lama. Very long trip. We got there and found their camp. Tents ripped to pieces. Blood everywhere. Ten college students and two faculty missing. They were dragged off into woods. Body parts torn off and eaten by something. Most gruesome thing I ever saw. Then, we find one college girl. Her legs had been torn off. She was still alive—just barely. She whispered something to me I never forget. And that is why I hope we not find a Yeti here in America."

Ranger Watson looked expectantly. "What did she ask?"

It was the governor who answered. "She wanted you to kill her?"

"Yes."

"Did you?"

"Yes. Uncle Ho wanted to spare young me but I told him I would take care of it. She was almost dead anyway. Colt Navy revolver easier than snapping neck."

"How long was she there?"

"Not sure. At least two weeks. British ambassador telegraphed Chinese government when they did not arrive. Two weeks lying on ground waiting for Yeti to come back and eat the rest of you."

"How could Yeti get here to America?"

"No idea," Ling Fung said. "If we find one, you can ask it."

"We'll all sleep good tonight," Ranger Watson added.

No one talked much after that. After about half an hour, Ling Fung continued, "We buried what was left of the people. That night we made camp. Too late to travel anywhere. About midnight we heard this howl coming from nearby woods. It was loud and certain it was meant for us. Horrible sound. Never forget it. Sort of sound that makes spine tingle."

"We don't have anything like that in Mexico. Not that I know of."

"Be thankful for that."

They made camp in a sheltered area near a grove of pine trees. There was no small fire this evening. Ling Fung hoped they wouldn't burn the forest down. "Man at newspaper said prospector cabin, or where it used to be, about another mile up the trail." Ranger Watson handed out some jerky.

"What's this?" the governor asked. "My teeth aren't what they once were. Not sure I can handle this. I miss my chef."

"Jerky. I don't go anywhere without some." He took a bite.

"Dog will take what you do not want."

Dog was intently watching them, hoping they might drop a piece of the dried meat.

As the night wore on, the men prepared their bedrolls. Everyone was staying close to the fire. Just as they were drifting off to sleep, the dog started growling.

"Can't someone shut him up?"

Ling Fung looked around. "Not like sound of this growl. Never heard it before." It was a deeper sound coming from the dog than his usual growl for something like a squirrel.

The governor crossed himself and said something in Spanish.

Out in the darkness, it was hard to tell how far, glowing red eyes cold be seen reflecting back the firelight. Then came a loud, almost deafening roar. Then, just as suddenly, whatever had been there was gone.

Ranger Watson rubbed the dog's ears. "Good boy. I'm glad we brought you."

They headed for where the prospector cabin once stood just after dawn. Ling Fung brought the Winchester repeater. "Many stories about Yeti, all through Asia. Some say he can even fly."

"You really think that's what we're up against?" Ranger Watson asked.

"Way Fong is curled up in a ball on floor of his tent. All he can say is Yeti."

"You didn't tell us that."

"Well, something was sure out there last night."

The famed prospector cabin was just a few rocks left over from the fireplace. Nature had reclaimed anything else that might have once been there. It didn't take long to find the entrance to a mine nearby. There was music coming from it. More accurately, there was a woman singing inside.

There were rugs on the floor. Various lanterns and a few candles lit up the interior, at least for twenty feet or so. And, someone had even installed a wood fired stove. The singing was coming from May Li. She poured some water into a tea cup, then dropped the pan and let out a shriek.

"I am Ling Fung. These gentlemen are your husbands."

And she stood there silently for a moment, then finally said something in Mandarin.

"She does not speak English. She wants us to leave." Ling Fung looked to his companions awaiting a response.

"Why?" Ranger Watson asked. "If'n you didn't want us for husbands, why put us through this?"

Ling Fung translated then awaited an answer. "She has a husband. And two of you paid better than just one. She says we are in great danger and should go now."

"We're in danger!"

"Ranger Watson, I believe we should leave."

Dog started growling.

"We must go now!"

They went outside the mine tunnel. A large rock struck Texas Ranger Todd Watson in the head, killing him instantly. "Holy mother of Jesus." Carlos de Bourbon, Governor of Chihuahua, Mexico crossed himself. "Are you going to use that rifle you've been carrying around?"

"It may only make him mad. We should head for the horses and hope he has not eaten them. That rock must weigh at least 25 pounds."

May Li started yelling something from the entrance to the mine cave.

Ling Fung replied in Mandarin. Then he repeated in English. "She thinks we are fools for even coming here. That may be so, but Texas Rangers will never stop trying to avenge their comrade."

"Not ever," the governor agreed. "They think my state is part of their jurisdiction. They'll come and keep coming."

"I told her as much. Mt. Lemmon too small an area to hide

in. I told her to go north into Rocky Mountains with her mate and never come back here."

"Who is her mate?" the governor asked.

Between their horses and them, stood a monster that was at least eight feet tall.  It was covered in a dirty white fur.  Its eyes were a reddish color.

"To answer your question." Ling Fung pointed at the monster. "Abominable Snowman. Yeti."

"She and that?"

"You just figure that out now?"

"I just wanted to be sure."

Then May Li started yelling again.  But her berate was not aimed at them.  The monster's shoulders sort of slumped down and he simply walked past them and into the mine entrance.

"Now, we must go."

Ranger Watson's body flew through the air and landed next to them.

"Guess we take body to sheriff. Doubt he will believe us."

"A Chinaman and a Mexican. Sure, the gringos will believe everything we tell them."

They headed back to Tombstone.  There were other towns in Arizona, but neither of them knew where they were.

"Your brother should give me my money back."

"Brother is a crook," Ling Fung replied. "At first I could not understand why I was here. I think brother thought I would kill you and Ranger Watson, then nobody is out any money. Nobody but Ling Fung."

The sheriff in Tombstone wrote down everything. He said he'd forward it to the U. S. Marshal in Prescott, the territorial capital, as Mt. Lemmon was not really in his jurisdiction.

Carlos returned to Mexico. It took Ling Fung a full week to get on a train heading back for California. Brother never did wire the funds for a ticket.

The entire event had been a pointless endeavor from Ling Fung's point of view. He noticed a lot of men wearing badges were riding into Tombstone as the train was leaving. It was a very long and tiring ride back to California. Dog had to ride in the baggage car.

# 3
## Home Sweet Home

Well, dog certainly seemed glad to get out of the baggage car. Ling Fung was just glad to be back from Arizona. The whole endeavor had been a waste of time and money. He did not appreciate brother's tactics. It had not occurred to him, until that very moment, to ask what was charged for May Li. He would probably never know.

He grabbed his carpet bag and headed for Main Street. "This is a horrible town. I do not like it here. I doubt you will, either," he explained to the dog. He looked at his reflection in the window of the local dry goods shop. "Wonder if I should get Stetson hat."

Dog did not offer any opinion on the matter.

"Perhaps wait and save money. Maybe we can someday go back to China. Whole country can't hate me." He started walking. "Probably can't all hate me. Uncle Ho say China not want me back. Not sure if that means everyone in whole country or just everyone in Guangdong. And Peking. And the Imperial Court. And Shaolin Temple probably still mad at me." He opened the door. "Are you potty trained? If not, poop in Lotus Blossom's room, not mine. "Where is brother?" Ling Fung asked.

"San Francisco," his insolent niece replied. "We were hoping you wouldn't come back."

"Nonetheless, I have returned."

"Where'd this dog come from?"

"Arizona."

"Why didn't you leave him there?"

"I would like something to eat. And fix something for the dog," he announced. He relaxed in the parlor. After considerable time, he ventured to the kitchen to see where his supper was. The kitchen was empty. There was no sign of Lotus Blossom anywhere. "Horrible child." Children in America did not know their place. He rummaged around and found a few items for himself and dog. Ling Fung was not really sure what dogs were supposed to eat. He'd never had one before. Thus far, the animal had devoured pretty much everything given to him. The bean curd he was eating was not a surprise. The dried papaya and the mushrooms had been unexpected. He prepared a bowl of water for him and returned to the parlor to read the *Mountain Democrat*.

Little had happened since he was gone. Curiously, there had never been any mention of the bird man in the newspaper. Ling Fung was not going to give up on the $20,000 in gold. Finally, he decided to go to bed.

"Dog, you sleep anywhere. If that horrible child returns, bite her." With that, he went to his room.

Around midnight the silence was interrupted. Dog was barking and someone was yelling in the parlor. Ling Fung staggered down the stairs to see what was causing so much commotion.

His brother, Ling Ming, was standing there holding the fireplace poker. Dog was growling and barking at him.

"Where did this dog come from?"

"Arizona." Ling Fung went back to bed and provided no further information. As he climbed back into bed he wondered if lotus Blossom had ever returned home. He decided he did not care.

Ling Fung was up early the next morning. All the traveling had messed up his internal timepiece. His external timepiece, in the form of a pocket watch removed from some gunfighter, said it was seven o'clock. His body was telling him it simply had to be later. Dog was asleep on the kitchen floor, snoring quite loudly. No one else seemed to be up yet. He headed off down Main Street.

The Honey Blossom Café was open. They offered fresh hot biscuits dripping in butter. He wondered why the Chinese hadn't invented something as wonderful as a biscuit. There was nothing equivalent that he could think of. Four biscuits, along with a link of sausage and cup of coffee seemed like a fine way to start a morning.

He headed back home when a sign in a window caught his eye. He was delighted the town marshal's office was already open.

"Help ya?" someone hovering over a stove asked.

"You have a sign in the window, deputy wanted."

"Yep."

"I was interested."

"I see." The man poured himself some coffee. "I'm Rip Jenkins, the town marshal."

"A pleasure to meet you. I am Ling Fung."

Rip took a seat behind his desk and gestured for Ling Fung to do likewise. "Now, frankly, I've often thought a Chinese deputy might be handy. We have the second largest Chinese population in northern California. Well, Mister Fung, it's like this."

"Actually, the Chinese place the surname in front. It's Ling. My common name is Fung."

"Okay. My last deputy just run off to Texas. They say the Texas Rangers are hiring like crazy." He took a sip of coffee. "Well then, Mister Ling. In California, Chinese aren't allowed to testify in court. You all are not trustworthy and are of a devious race. Not my words. That is the official policy of the California State Assembly." He took a sip of coffee. 'Well, having a deputy who couldn't actually testify in court, well I don't see that working out too well."

"Thank you for your time."

"Nothing personal."

Ling Fung stood.

"Oh, one other thing," Rip Jenkins said. "Is your brother a crook?"

"That seems a bit impertinent."

"Well, folks come in here all the time telling me he's a crook. Just thought I'd ask."

"I do not know. But, in all likelihood, he probably is. Good morning." Ling Fung headed out the door. So much for securing gainful employment on this day.

He picked up a copy of the *Mountain Democrat* which he took home and seated himself in the parlor. He could hear Lotus Blossom arguing with his brother upstairs, although he could not follow the precise conversation.

Dog soon found him. Apparently, dog needed his ears rubbed.

It turned out Lotus Blossom went to the laundry and worked there for a few hours. This was not unusual. It was a family business. Curiously, no one had ever asked Ling Fung to work in there.

It turned out dog liked egg drop soup. He also devoured a few cups of fried rice. That was what Ling Fung cooked for supper. It was a shame white people were generally afraid of Chinese food. Ling Fung had envisioned going to San Francisco and opening up a restaurant. And lines of white people would wait just to get a table. But he knew the Chinese residents of Placerville seldom ate in restaurants and were not likely to pay him to cook for them. His only customer would be dog and dog did not seem to have any money.

He and dog went to his room and looked over the arsenal. There were eight Winchester repeaters that had been taken away from white men, an assortment of knives and even a silver throwing hatchet he had taken away from one of the tong enforcers. "Won't be long and we can open our own gun store," he told dog.

There was also a revolver, manufactured by the Milton Purdy Company of Chicago, Illinois. It was a plain and simple weapon with ordinary wood handles and an unremarkable blue finish with no engravings of any kind, save for the name of the company. Even that was in plain simple type. That particular weapon was of interest mainly because no one had ever heard of the manufacturer and he could not find any ammunition for it. It appeared to take a .40 caliber shell. Nothing in that size seemed to exist that would even come close to fitting. Since he'd taken the gun away from somebody, he had no idea if there still were dealers carrying this company's products. He put the weapons back inside the closet.

"That dog has to sleep outside," Lotus Blossom announced.

"Why is that?"

"My father does not want him in the house. He snores."

"My brother does not snore," Ling Fung insisted.

"No, the dog does."

"Well, that is a matter between you and dog. I am going to bed." With that, he closed the door to his room. He could hear considerable growling and then all was quiet. A half hour later he could hear snoring coming from someplace down the hall. Then the snoring stopped.  He could hear the slop, slop, slop of dog drinking from the water bowl all the way down in the kitchen. Sounds really carry in a quiet house at night.

# 4
## SELF-EMPLOYMENT

How difficult could bounty hunting be?

Rip Jenkins shook his head and went inside the office. Ling Fung followed him.

"People don't take into account travel expenses. They just see that five hundred dollar reward and they go nuts. Truth is, it's not that easy tracking down folks who don't want to be found. Most rewards are never collected. Coffee?"

Ling Fung accepted a cup. He was slowly developing a taste for American coffee, most of which came from South America. He thought of going back home and growing and selling coffee. Since he came from a nation of tea drinkers, he doubted that would be successful—not to mention the Emperor had ordered his execution. He couldn't picture the Emperor drinking coffee. Perhaps if the can had a picture of him in a hangman's noose. Dead Man Fung's Gourmet Blend might prove popular in the royal court. And it always was served in blue cups that had little speckles on them. He thought about asking Marshal Jenkins why it was always served that way, then decided not to. He was there for business. "So you have a wanted poster for five hundred dollars then?" That was a considerable amount of money. He and dog could certainly open up a gun store with that.

"Nope. Look, the only wanted poster I got is for Smoky Joe Franklin." He fumbled around in a file cabinet for a few minutes. "Now, Smoky Joe lives in a cabin about ten miles east of here, well outside the municipal boundary of this town. I have no interest in going and arresting him. And our beloved county sheriff displays a similar lack of enthusiasm. It's a Sacramento warrant. Let Sacramento come and fetch him." He removed a rolled up parchment from the cabinet. "Fifty dollar bounty for theft. No idea what he stole."

He unrolled the poster on his desktop. "Ugly feller. Truth is, most wanted posters ain't really designed to get a fugitive back."

"Then why?"

"To keep them away. Smoky Joe Franklin ain't likely to go back to Sacramento 'cause there's a bounty on his head. And, truth be known, Sacramento is happy with that."

Ling Fung thought about his own predicament. China didn't want him back and said as much. But there was no reward, in his own situation, just a promised execution if he showed up in the country again. "I'll go and apprehend this man."

Rip handed him the poster. "Suit yourself."

Ling Fung went to the livery and retrieved his horse. Then he went by the house and gathered food for a few days. He told dog, "We're going to go and take another gun away from a white man."

As they headed out of town he noticed a young Chinese man standing on the wooden sidewalk trying hard not to be noticed. "Man over there bring trouble. Wonder if he's here for me or Ming. Probably crooked brother. You have not done anything have you?"

Dog did not answer.

A small hatchet suddenly came flying tough the air. Ling Fung grabbed it right out of the air. "Well, I guess we'll have a section in gun store for knives and hatchets." He drew his Colt Navy revolver and cocked the hammer. The fellow was already halfway down the street. Curiously, dog was chasing him.

Ling Fung galloped the horse after him. When he caught up, a snarling dog had the man cornered, of sorts, on his knees on top of the public outhouse. "Dog, dog come here."

"How'd you train him to come after me?"

"Small matter. Bigger matter, why should I not kill you here and now?"

"Look, I just do what they tell me."

"Of course you do. Come along, dog." And they headed for the road out of town.

Ling Fung looked over his new silver hatchet. This was not a weapon for cutting wood. It was a weapon designed for throwing. "Yes, we will soon have plenty of inventory for gun and knife store." *And who taught dog how to run down somebody like that?* he wondered.

He slid the hatchet down into his saddle bag. The Chinese tongs loved to use hatchets. While they were not always the most efficient weapons, the sight of someone with a hatchet sticking out of his head was a powerful and instant symbol of their authority.

But, first things first. They had bounty hunter work to tend to. The tong would still be there when they got back.

This was the first time Ling Fung hadn't been cold. It was a nice night. There was no wind and they had a full moon. He decided to make camp. That way they could affect an arrest in the morning and he wouldn't have to worry about guarding a prisoner all night.

Dog ate his soy beans. That seemed odd. Essentially, dog seemed to eat everything. Dogs were supposed to be carnivores, not omnivores like bears. Of course, no one cooked soybeans like Ling Fung. Americans were too afraid to season anything.

He unrolled his bedroll and stretched out. There stars were out. It was a truly nice night out. The sort of night a man might think he didn't have a care in the world.

"Grrr."

"We were here, minding our own business. Apparently, we are about to be disturbed."

Dog was fixated on the area where the horse was tied up.

"Logical, to prevent our escape."

A hatchet swirled out of the darkness as its distinctive whoop, whoop, whoop fought the quiet of the night. Ling Fung grabbed it out of the air and tossed it on his bedroll. Another hatchet came out of the darkness behind him. He grabbed that as well. "Show yourself." He repeated in Mandarin.

He noticed dog was no longer in the camp. There was no time to look for him. Ling Fung took the crane stance.

A few seconds later a man came out of the darkness. He was wearing golden colored silk robes. Ling Fung had seen these before, although he knew little about them or their owners. "Show me your arms," his opponent demanded. The opponent was surprisingly young, probably no more than sixteen. "Show me your arms."

"I have nothing to show you."

"They say you are Shaolin."

"I have never said that."

"Then show me your arms. Shaolin mark their arms."

"You can examine my arms after I am dead." This warranted a change. He took the tiger stance.

"Very well," his opponent said.

Ling Fung had never dropped the second hatchet. He threw it at his opponent. The hatchet sailed through the air and harmlessly went by the fighter. A second later a shuriken tore into his throat. It was always amazing how many adversaries failed to observe he was left handed and the throwing star was often on its way before anyone noticed.

Now where was the second adversary? That was answered as another man entered the camp, this one was older—about the same age as Ling Fung. He also wore the same sort of golden robes.

"Your companion is dead, yet I still do not know why we are fighting."

"Are you Shaolin?"

Ling Fung was tiring of this. He unbuttoned the sleeves of his shirt. "As you can plainly see, there are no animals burned into my arms. Whatever quarrel you have with the Shaolin, you are on the wrong continent."

"You fight like them."

"There are many schools of fighting throughout Asia."

"True enough." He moved into a fighting stance. Ling Fung had seen it before. And it was not in China.

"And your master owes me $200,000 in gold and one very good horse."

The assailant shrugged. "Take it up with him. After you die."

A few of the men at the Owl Mine had demonstrated tactics of Asian martial arts and an unusual fighting stance he now recognized. Ling Fung had not been impressed. They certainly were no match for years of training at a Shaolin temple. He resumed his crane stance.

His adversary charged him. The crane, one of five animals Kung Fu emulates, was most effective against a charging enemy. Wherever bird man was recruiting these guys from, he really could do a little better.

"Now where is dog? Fight over."

Dog came running back into the camp. He hit Ling Fung so hard they both landed on the ground. When the animal stopped licking him, Ling Fung helped himself up. "Yes, I was worried about you, too. Let's leave these two for buzzards. Camp somewhere else."

# 5
## CRIMINALS

Ling Fung wondered why he was called Smoky Joe Franklin. A steady stream of gray smoke had been gently wafting out of the chimney of the one room shack since they'd arrived. It certainly was not unusual to heat one's home, or simply to prepare a pot of coffee. Since he was new to the profession of bounty hunting, he was not certain about the accepted protocol of going about these things. He did not wish to make a poor impression on his first arrest.

The assailants from the previous night had broken many rules. One does not enter someone's camp in the middle of the night. It was unthinkable. Unless you're a Japanese Ninja, who are assassins and have their own code. Here in America, everything seemed different. No manners, no self-discipline. Well, he would take the matter up with Ah Puch at a future date. For now, Smoky Joe Franklin was his concern. "Wait with horse, dog. Don't let him steal horse. Don't want to walk all the way back home."

He knocked on the door. He waited a few seconds, then knocked again.

The door opened, just a crack. "Yeah?"

"Good morning. I am Ling Fung." He unrolled the wanted poster.

The door slammed shut. It appeared to have a good, solid lock on it.

"Now, this not a high amount of reward. You certainly should open the door. I do not wish to use force against you, Mister Franklin."

Nothing happened.

He kicked the door. It was quite solid. Still, it was not so solid that a few well placed kicks of Chinese Kung Fu could not handle. There was a bed and little else in front. He found a second room, what would normally pass for a kitchen. Most of this space was taken up with a large smoke box. This was obviously what had been generating the smoke coming from the cabin. He opened the door. There were racks filled with smoking meats. Ribs were at the bottom, other cuts higher up. A small fire churned out smoke from a cylinder at the base. There was a bowl of some sort of brine solution on a table, as well as some tongs and a basting brush.

"Now we know why they call him Smoky Joe Franklin," Ling Fung told an empty room. The process of preserving meats by smoking them was quite common in America. It was not done to a large extent where he was from. He opened a rear door that went outside. There was an awning and a porch. And more meat. At least, Ling Fung was able to figure out what had been cooking inside. Two human bodies were on tables. They had been gutted and quartered, apparently just about ready for smoking. "So this is the secret to American barbecue."

A bullet ricocheted off the awning. "Apparently, this man wants to try smoking Chinese food." The report of another round from a rifle rang out from somewhere up the hill behind the cabin.

"Yah! Get this dog off me."

Ling Fung took immediate advantage of the distraction and advanced up the hill. Smoky Joe Franklin was stumbling down the hill trying to keep dog away with the butt of a rifle while trying to reload the same rifle. He aimed his Navy Colt and yelled, "Okay dog, I'll take it from here."

Dog continued to growl, but stopped trying to bite the fugitive.

"Mister, you got me." After he was properly tied up and they were riding back toward town, Smoky Joe said, "Never figured on no Chinee bounty hunter."

"Since they completed the railroad, many of us have had to take up other trades."

They rode on into Placerville. Rip Jenkins gave them a funny look. "Look Fung, I said you have to take him over to Sacramento to get your bounty."

"I am not hard of hearing, Marshal. Please come with us." He parked the horses in front of the County Jail and Office of the El Dorado County Sheriff. He helped Smoky Joe off his horse and led him inside.

Sheriff Thurmond Thomas and a deputy looked up from their blue speckled coffee mugs. "What have we here?"

"This is Ling Fung," Marshal Jenkins explained. "He's taken up bounty hunting. Smoky Joe Franklin had a bounty out of Sacramento."

"A low one, as I recall," the sheriff replied. "Why bring him here? I don't want him."

"You may not want him, but you get him nonetheless," Ling Fung explained.

"How so?"

"This man smokes unusual meats."

"Heck, we all know that. That's why he's called Smoky Joe."

"This man has been smoking human body parts at his cabin. The house is a smoker and mortuary all rolled into one. There are two freshly killed bodies on the back porch that are draining and drying as we speak."

"You remember what I told you about Chinese testifying in court?" Marshal Jenkins asked.

"Of course." Ling Fung went out to the horses, removed two items wrapped in paper, then came back inside. "Whether I testify or not, if you should ride up to his cabin you will find cooked people." He unrolled the first parcel. A shiny oblong item dropped out. "Human sausage." He unwrapped the second parcel. "Smoked foot and leg." He dropped it on the desk in front of Sheriff Thomas.

The deputy fled outside and threw up on the sidewalk. "Oh God," he yelled before throwing up again.

Sheriff Thomas placed Smoky Joe in a cell. "Of course, we'll go ride up there and check this out. Deputy Hatcher, when you're through soiling the public sidewalk go and fetch Deputy Wainwright. You want to come along Rip."

"I don't know if I want to, but I think I ought to."

"Good day, gentlemen. Come along dog," Ling Fung said.

"Who let that dog in here?"

By late afternoon an article appeared in the *Mountain Democrat* with a bold headline reading **LOCAL CANNIBAL ARRESTED**. There was no mention of Ling Fung or any local citizen. One would think that Sheriff Thomas, who was up for re-election, had solved the matter singlehandedly.

Ling Fung drank the last of his stash of Chinese beer. He couldn't seem to get the smell of the smoked bodies to go away. Even with fresh clothes and a bath, everything still smelled like the smokehouse.

He put the paper down and looked over at dog, who had also undergone a bath. "Only good thing out of this is he had a Sharp's rifle. I've wanted one of those. Our inventory just keeps on growing."

"Erf."

Marshal Jenkins came up the steps and handed Ling Fung fifty dollars.

"What is this for?"

"I wired Sacramento. I served the warrant for them. So you get the reward. He'll never go to trial for a theft charge, not with all he's facing. Heck, we're not even sure how many dead bodies he cooked up." He looked around to see if anyone was listening. "Heck, Smokey Joe apparently sold Curtis, over at the butcher shop some sausages. I'm not going to be eating sausages for a very long time."

"They are not common in Chinese food, Marshal. Still, I'll make a point of avoiding them." He put the money away in his pocket.

# 6
## INDUSTRY

The next day was quite pleasant outside. Ling Fung found himself relaxing on the front porch. Few people in the Chinese part of town read the newspaper. That was mainly due to the fact they couldn't read English. The Jesuits, before they kicked him out, had taught him many things that were quite useful in the world controlled by white men. For instance, brother's math skills were not quite so good. He had not noticed money was disappearing from the laundry. He'd spent the morning going over the books. The discrepancies were obvious. He thought brother might try going back to an abacus. When European colonial powers in places like Hong Kong had introduced western notions of bookkeeping, it had been a disaster. Five thousand years of using an abacus was a tough habit to break. However, brother was not particularly good with an abacus, either.

Now, he had found a crooked employee and it was not even lunch time. Lotus Blossom came back from the store, where she had picked up the mail. Most of it was for brother, but she handed him a letter. It was coming all the way from Chicago. It was from the Milton Purdy Company. Ling Fung had been writing to firearms makers trying to secure distribution when he finally opened his gun store. Somehow, his Chinese name seemed to result in few responses. They were the company that he had acquired two pistols manufactured by them, but there was no ammunition to be had anywhere in the state.

*Dear Mr. Fung:*

A common mistake. It should be Mr. Ling, but no matter.

*Thank you for writing us about the lack of ammunition. We ship a good supply of our .40 caliber pistol ammunition each month. Still,*

*we often receive complaints such as yours. We are investigating the matter and confident the problem will soon be resolved.*
Arnold Schultz
*Vice President*


That was nice of them to write. But they did not offer him any solution to the problem. A revolver from this company was only good as a hammer or, perhaps, for cracking walnuts.

He took a sip of tea. Crooked employee, one Chow Fat, came running by the house. Brother appeared to be chasing him with a knife in his hand. This could get exciting. Then, out of nowhere, two deputy town marshals ended the altercation and took both men off to jail. "Marshals probably can't understand Chinese and have no idea what dispute is about," he explained to dog.

Dog didn't seem much more interested in the whole affair than Ling Fung was.

He took another sip of tea and went back to reading the newspaper. They went inside when it started getting dark. He lit a few lamps. His brother was such a crook it sort of served him right that he was being stolen from.

Ling Fung found some food in the kitchen for dog. It seemed odd that dog liked soup and rice. He did not recall seeing dogs eat such things. That turned out to be what he ate as well. He was putting plates away when Lotus Blossom appeared.

"My father is in jail."

"I know that."

"Then, why don't you do something?"

"Because Marshal doesn't work nights. He will be in his office in morning. I will go over and see what your father is charged with. It is likely a big mistake. You must understand, Americans don't always understand our way of life. It takes patience sometimes."

"Oh."

He retired to his room for the evening. After taking his shoes off, he unfolded and read the letter again from the Milton Purdy Company. It would be nice if he could obtain some ammunition. That was always the problem with firearms. The

patent laws let manufacturers control the ammunition to them.
A .45 long Colt was incompatible with a .45. His own Navy
Colt used a .36 caliber bullet that was seldom easy to find. And
firearms companies were constantly going out of business. And
Smoky Joe had .40 caliber ammunition in his cabin. The Sharps
rifle he took used a .50 caliber bullet. It was a hunting weapon,
after all. So why was there a box of .40 ammunition in that cabin? Why was there Milton Purdy Ammunition in that cabin?
This would have to be looked into.

❧

*One of the younger students who tended the candles woke him.
It was very dark in the dormitory. Only a few candles lit the room.
"Master Wu wants you."*

*Ling Fung sat up. "Okay. Where is he?"*

*"The pond."*

*Of course. Master Wu was always down at the pond. Ling Fung
approached as quietly as he could. It was impossible to sneak up on
Master Wu. Yet he kept trying.*

*"We have discussed your situation with us."*

*Ling Fung sat down beside his master. "Yes, Master?"*

*"You have come a long way. Your fighting skills are remarkable,
perhaps the best I have ever seen. But there is more to being a Shaolin
monk than simply fighting."*

*"All the lessons, the teachings of The Sage. I know."*

*"We are troubled by what happened yesterday."*

*"The bandits. They wanted the wagon of food, our food."*

*"Yes, I heard your account yesterday. And five armed bandits
now lie dead along the side of the road to Guangdong."*

*"Am I to allow anyone to attack me at will, Master?"*

*"They only wanted a few vegetables. You, yourself, were not in
any real danger."*

*"No, not really," he agreed.*

*"Is a man's life worth more than a few vegetables? Even a ban-
dit?"*

*"It does not seem in my nature to passively yield to those who
would attack me, Master."*

*"You have become too proficient in the art of killing. It is time
for you to leave."*

*"I'm not sure I understand, Master?" The question was pointless.*

*He was now alone at the pond.*

Ling Fung sat up in bed. He had not thought of the monastery in a long time. The hatchet bearers, they had recognized his fighting style. They suspected he was Shaolin. What could he tell them? I'm Shaolin, but I'm not?

Living in America, his training was irrelevant. All Chinese looked alike. All Asian martial arts looked alike. But, to an experienced eye, the style of fighting was all important.

Dog was snoring in the hallway outside. He soon drifted off to sleep again.

# 7
## BULLETS

The scrambled eggs were delicious that morning. One of the benefits of having a few chickens. Fresh eggs made so much difference. And cooking them yourself. Lotus Blossom always burned everything. That dreadful old woman who cleaned the house, everything she cooked was dry and overdone. "If you want something done right, do it yourself."

"What was that?" Lotus Blossom asked.

"Nothing." He hadn't been talking to her. Dog understood. Dog liked Ling Fung's scrambled eggs. He did not care if the child enjoyed their amazing flavor or not.

"How come he doesn't have a name?"

"Who doesn't have a name?"

"That mutt."

"How do you know he doesn't have a name?"

"Well, if he does, no one seems to know what it is."

"Precisely. The dog has not told me what his name is. That does not mean he does not have one." Master Wu would have been proud. Anyone else would have named the dog.

"That is ridiculous."

"Eat your eggs." The biscuits weren't half bad, either. That was one American invention he approved of. Today he was using apricot jelly. But honey or even just butter all worked. And biscuits went with nearly everything. And they were easy to prepare if you had a hot stove or oven going. He didn't recall anything like them in China. And his were the best. Maybe he could sell biscuits along with guns. Something seemed odd with that.

He noticed the child was gone. He wondered if she went to school or worked down in the laundry all day. He'd have to find out. It didn't matter so much as she was crooked brother's kid, but he was thinking he should know these things. They didn't have women at the Shaolin monastery. For that matter, the Jesuit mission in Guangdong didn't have women either. That had always seemed like a good thing. Although he was wondering if women get an education. He would have to find out. Perhaps they could send Lotus Blossom far away to a boarding school someplace. He'd heard of such things, although he did not understand how they worked.

Ling Fung had not really understood how the Shaolin monastery selected its students. Uncle Ho had dropped him off one day and said he would come back at the end of the day. But, instead, he found himself being invited inside the monastery. Even so many years later he still had no idea how their selection process worked. He would likely never know since they kicked him out. Since Lotus Blossom was too old to start training at a Shaolin monastery, sending her there would be pointless. And the fact she was a girl. He'd heard rumors now and then that another Shaolin monastery actually took girls and even taught them Kung Fu. He suspected that may have been idle talk when some of the priests enjoyed a little too much of the rice wine. Another mystery that would remain unsolved.

He put some more jelly on the last biscuit, then handed it to dog. The biscuit vanished in a second. "Do you bother to taste how good and wonderful my biscuits are?"

The dog stared blankly back at him.

"There are no more. Breakfast is now over. Time to go see why brother is in jail."

☯

Rip Jenkins was staring blankly at the coffee pot. Ling Fung was unsure if it was communicating with the town marshal or the marshal was somehow hoping that it would be ready faster if he continued staring at it.

"My brother is in jail." Ling Fung took a vacant chair. "May I ask why?"

"Brandishing a deadly weapon." He poured some coffee into his blue and white cup then took his seat behind his desk. "He was running around Main Street waving a knife around."

"Well, more specially, he was waving it at Chow Fat, who my brother discovered has been stealing money at his laundry business."

"Oh."

"I guess getting stolen from does tend to rile up a man."

"Yes, it has been known to happen."

"This Chow Fat, well my deputies didn't fully understand the situation. He seems to have run off somewhere. How does this sound? I'll release your brother." He looked at a blotter on his desk. "Ling Ming, and we'll forget that matter entirely."

"An excellent solution."

Rip went back into the jail area and soon returned with his brother.

They were halfway home before Ming said anything. "You enjoyed that, didn't you?"

"Confucius say 'why kill when you can take his money instead?'"

"He never said that."

"Well, I may have forgotten the exact quote. But you have a week's unpaid wages, which is likely worth nearly as much as he stole from you. Did they feed you breakfast?"

"I don't like American food," Ming said. "Something called flapjacks."

"I love those. So, you even got a free meal out of this."

"You are starting to love this country too much."

"Brother, it is the country I have left. The Emperor of China has decreed I should be put to death."

Ming smiled for just a moment at the thought of seeing his brother executed. "And the Jesuits have excommunicated you and damned your soul to hell. You do seem to be running out of options."

"Perhaps so."

"Ling May is probably worried. Did she go to school today?"

"Yes, I believe she did." Ling Fung, in truth, had no idea where she went. He didn't even know if there was a school in this horrible town. He'd almost forgotten her real name as he always called her Lotus Blossom.

There was a white man sitting on the porch of the house. Ling Fung did not recognize him.

"I'll go see if my business is still there. Why don't you see what this white man wants," Ling Ming suggested.

That seemed like a plan. "May I help you?"

"Hello, there didn't seem to be anyone home. I am looking

for Ling Fung."

"Well, you are no longer looking. You have found him."

"You wrote our company. I'm here to follow up." He extended a hand. "Name's Purdy, Milton Purdy, president of the Milton Purdy Company."

"Would you like to come inside?" Ling Fung asked.

"Thank you." He followed him inside. Purdy was wearing a standard business suit and carried a large red carpet bag.

"Mister Purdy, I'm a little surprised you would come all the way from Chicago simply because I wrote you a letter. Would you like some tea?"

"Yes, thank you."

That was surprising. White people did not usually go for tea—at least not Americans. And there was nothing but Midwest America in his accent. He should've offered coffee. That was the wretched swill Americans gulped down. Percolation? What a wretched way to prepare a beverage.

"In China, only those in the royal court were once allowed to consume tea." He handed his visitor a cup. "Of course, that was a long time ago." Ling Fung poured some for himself. "So, how may I help you, Mister Purdy?"

"All the ammo we ship out west, well it just sort of disappears. We send cars full of ammunition on the railroads and it never arrives. Folks can't shoot our guns 'cause there ain't no ammo."

"Where does it go, exactly?" Ling Fung asked.

"It gets delivered. It's paid for. We ship it to some address in Oakland, or here in Placerville and it's never seen again. Yet no one appears to be missing it."

"Well, I don't see how I can help you?"

"Marshal Jenkins recommended I see you. He said there's no evidence of a crime, so there is nothing he can do."

"Well, I tend to agree there is little that can be done." Ling Fung sipped his tea for a moment. "When does the next shipment arrive?"

"It arrives in two days in Stockton. I must know who is trying to ruin my company."

"Odd, that buying up all of your product is ruining your company."

"No one will buy our guns. Eventually these orders will disappear and we will be left without any customers at all." He went over to the carpet bag and opened it. "I can offer you this brand new revolver with 250 rounds of ammunition for your trouble. And you can keep half of whatever ammunition you are able to recover."

"If it is lawfully purchased, I do not see how I can recover any of it."

"Well, I must know what is happening to it. I'll guarantee you five hundred dollars. That's not bad for two days' work."

"Agreed." Ling Fung held up the revolver so dog could see it. "Another revolver." He put the weapon down and finished drinking his tea. "I will leave for Stockton right away."

# 8
## GHOST TOWNS

*Lord Montgomery shouted at the driver. "Damn you, just run these blasted people down. We haven't got all day!"*

*The wagon driver tried to get around the slow moving old woman, but there was very little room. Eventually they were clear of her.*

*Ling Fung was sitting in back and had limited view of the situation. The Tibetans weren't really that keen on Chinese, probably even less so than these blasted British. This job had given him an opportunity to quickly get out of China and he had availed himself of it.*

*He'd recommended camels for the journey. Of course, they were being pulled by oxen which were much cheaper. It may not have mattered. At 12,000 feet elevation, beasts of burden labored just as men did. And the road continued even higher into the Himalayas.*

*"Mister Ling, it's getting damned cold at night," Major Wentworth said. He was sitting next to him in the crowded wagon.*

*"We are over 12,000 feet in elevation. The hot days we saw are behind us. There is a Buddhist monastery a few more miles ahead. Hopefully we can stay there tonight."*

*"Right o."*

*How did he know there was a monastery? He read the map. Ling Fung had a map written in Chinese. Few of the locals could read Chinese. Even fewer would admit knowing how if asked. He was the only one who could read the maps in the trunk he was sitting on. Oh Britannia.*

*Major Kevin Wentworth, retired, of the British Royal Army, wasn't so bad, save for his penchant to tell war stories around the campfire. It was Lord Trevor Montgomery who was going to get them all killed. In a town of at least 10,000 Tibetans, and he's yelling to run some woman over. These were not the streets of Calcutta. These people did not like foreigners and there were a lot more of them than his little band of three white men and six Sherpa porters.*

*The third white man was Sergeant Major William Smith, also retired. He spoke little. He didn't seem to like any oriental and did not really differentiate between a Chinaman and a Tibetan. At least he was transparent about it.*

The Abbott at the monastery agreed they could spend the night. Ling Fung was surprised he was given his own room. The monks entertained them with a welcoming ceremony. Then the group was fed supper.

The sergeant major did not look at all pleased with the fare at the table. "There's no meat on any of this."

"Buddhist monks are vegetarians," Ling Fung tried to explain. He scooped a tofu dish onto the sergeant major's plate. "Try some of this."

He filled his own plate. He had not had a banquet of this caliber in a very long time. In fact, before he came across the British he had been reduced to eating grubs and rats. Still, he was strangely pleased to see the sergeant major was actually eating the food.

After supper, Ling Fung was very pleased to retire the room he'd been given. He feared it might be the last good night's rest he was going to get. He hated the cold. And it was getting noticeably colder every single night.

A few minutes later there was a knock at the door. He was surprised to see the Abbott standing there. He gestured for him to come in. "Father Abbott I must thank you for your generous hospitality."

"I am not referred to as father."

"Of course not." A ridiculous mistake for someone who had nearly become a Shaolin priest. "I spent some time with the Jesuits in Hong Kong."

"Ah. That surprises me. I would have almost thought you had some training in our religion. No matter. It would be impolite for me to ask your companions what your destination is?"

"I think you already know. Why else would British come all this way?"

"I feared as much. Well, others have come before and never found it."

"They asked for my help in guiding them here and in translating for them. Their motives have not been revealed, though I would imagine they are treasure seekers as most westerners are."

"Yes, I tend to agree. Do you seek treasure for yourself?"

"No," Ling Fung assured him. "Although I was curious. One cannot help but be curious if Shambhala really exists."

"Good night," the Abbott suddenly said. "Pleasant journeys. I am no longer worried." As he walked away the Abbott added, "We have never had a Shaolin here."

For a long time, perhaps several hours, Ling Fung lay awake wondering how he could have possibly known he had been involved with the Shaolin. He finally fell asleep.

The next morning they were underway. They'd traveled five miles from the temple. The road appeared to turn off to the left. "Go right," Ling Fung insisted.

They turned off onto what seemed more like an animal trail. They rode along, bouncing and jostling, for most of the day. Then they came to a river that was too deep for the wagons to cross. Although there were rocks which enabled one to step across without getting wet.

"May I suggest," Ling Fung said as he read the map, "that the Sherpas set up camp here. We should go ahead on foot."

"For how far?" the sergeant major asked.

"It should be just over that hill."

Ling Fung noticed Major Wentworth placed a revolver underneath his jacket. Sure you're funded by Oxford University. Sure you are.

So, the four of them set out. And, as soon as they crested the hill on the other side of the river, they saw a large area carved out with at least a hundred rooms cut out. They appeared interconnected. They quickly found very old paintings on the wall. And statues that were very very old.

"Do you have any idea how much the British Museum will pay for this stuff?" the sergeant major asked no one in particular.

They looked around for a while. "Gentlemen, there are many wonders and treasures here. And we could explore this village for weeks. However, you have paid me to get you to the lost city of Shambhala. I have now figured out where the entrance is."

"Take us there," the sergeant major insisted.

They went to the very end of the village. There was a tunnel that was only slightly larger than the entrances to the other rooms and tunnels on the side of the cliff. "It is through there."

"We're gonna be rich," the sergeant major said.

"Aren't you coming?" Lord Montgomery asked.

"Legend has it that only those who are pure of heart and have a clean mind may enter Shambhala. I urge you not to go any further."

"Do you have a clean mind, Mister Ling?"

*"No, I do not."*
*"Then go back to camp. We don't need you anymore."*
*"As you wish."*

☯

Ling Fung sat up in bed. His heart was racing. He was covered in sweat. He looked around. He was still in the Woo family's house in Stockton. Dog was asleep on the floor. Everything was as it should be. He wondered why he'd dreamt of Shambhala. It had been such a long time. He would never get the screams of those men out of his mind.

The Woo family had allowed him to stay with them before. In fact, he had a sense of obligation towards them as they had helped him when he first arrived in the United States. Although Ling Fung spoke and read English, thanks to the Jesuit brothers in Hong Kong, Ling Fung, like most arrivals to a strange land, appreciated having a place to stay.

They were not altruistic, however, as Grandmother Woo seemed very determined to find a husband for her granddaughter. Alas, Bo was about the homeliest woman Ling Fung had come across in his entire life. And you couldn't really counter that with other qualities, as she didn't seem to have any. She openly farted at the dinner table. She snored worse than dog. And she smelled funny. Marrying Woo Bo was simply too much to ask. And, the other gentlemen of Chinatown felt pretty much the same.

Grandmother Woo was not stupid or naive. She realized no one would marry the girl unless he had a gun to his head or was otherwise in some way insane or mentally feeble. So she'd recently taken to trying to find a white husband for the girl. Had the girl been born a decade earlier, when there were very few women in the state and plenty of lonely railroad men, well things might have worked out. As it was, the white men were not showing much interest in her either.

So, Ling Fung found himself in the parlor with Grandmother Woo in another one of those awkward situations that had become the price for a night's lodging when passing through Stockton.

"You have a dog, now."

"Yes ma'am. I've had him about six months."

"Have you found any likely prospects for my granddaughter? She is not getting any younger?"

"Grandmother Woo, the truth is, I recently met a gentleman in Placerville who might be a suitable candidate. In fact, it is on his business that I am here in Stockton today. When I return, I will try and find a way to make an introduction."

"Is this a white gentleman?"

"Alas, Grandmother Woo, the men in Placerville are no more interested in Bo than are the men here in Stockton. After the 4th of July, she tried to shoot the town marshal. Well, things like that are not quickly forgotten. And she is still most unwelcome there."

"She actually does not drink so much anymore."

"I'm glad to hear that. No, the gentleman I have in mind is Milton Purdy. He is from Chicago and knows nothing of your granddaughter's affection for rice wine. And he has his own business."

"You have done well," she declared.

"Now, I must tend to some business this morning," Ling Fung said. He clapped his hand. "Come along dog."

The ship arrived at the Port of Stockton just as it should have. Various boxes and barrels were unloaded by the longshoremen. Some of the goods were placed on wagons. Other items that weren't being immediately claimed were placed in a nearby warehouse. Therein was the problem. It was not easy to distinguish one shipment from another.

One wagon caught his eye. It wasn't the cargo so much as its recipients. All three men were wearing gray shirts and pants as if they were Civil War rejects. "What is it about gray outfits with these guys?"

Dog did not seem to know. In fact, dog appeared to be asleep.

The three men climbed on board the buckboard and headed down the road that went out of town on the road to Sacramento. Buckboards were slow and noisy, and tended to kick up a lot of dust. This made following one relatively easy. Ling Fung was pleased to note that dog was trotting alongside his horse. "I would have hated for you to have had to spend the rest of your life here in Stockton with Woo Bo. She might get drunk and shoot you. That is what happened to her last dog. And the one before that. Although Grandmother Woo assures me the girl is drinking less now." Dog did not seem to be paying attention.

It was not long before the buckboard turned off the main road and went off toward a ranch. "Double Owl Ranch? Doesn't anyone ever notice things like this? Come dog, maybe we can get more guns for our store."

But there were no guns. There were no guys in gray. There wasn't even a wagon. The place didn't look like it had seen much activity in years. The ranch house was deserted. The barn was deserted. Wherever the shipment of ammunition had gone, it certainly could not be found.

"Well, dog, I guess we might as well go home."

Dog, apparently had other ideas. He ran around behind the ranch house with his nose just above the ground. He followed some kind of scent over to the windmill, then he stopped at a pile of brush.

It took a minute for Ling Fung to catch up. "A tunnel. They fooled the dumb Chinaman, but they didn't fool the dog." At the entrance to the tunnel was an oil lamp and a box of matches. "Even better. Bats, I mean owls, may like the dark but Ling Fung does not."

They went about fifty yards down into the secret tunnel when they found the wagon, still loaded with ammunition. Unfortunately, the team had been unhitched. Without horses, simply riding off with ammunition, which is extremely heavy, would simply be impossible. They continued farther down into the tunnel.

In a few minutes they came upon an open cavern area. It was not apparent whether this was a natural formation or manmade. Although he didn't see anyone around, a familiar whooshing sound broke the silence. He plucked it out of the air. "Could you not throw something else at me? I really am not in need of any more hatchets."

A shadow could be seen where the hatchet came from. Slowly, Ah Puch moved out into the light. "I thought your people liked hatchets."

"It is true that some tongs dismember people with them,

on rare occasion. The hatchet is more for intimidation. As a fighting weapon, there are better choices." Ling Fung moved out of the way of a shuriken.

"Is that a better choice?" Ah Puch asked. "I was so intrigued with these I had a set made for me."

"I have all of them I need. Perhaps you could throw gold coins at me?"

"Most men who are brought before me cower or plead for their lives. If we were back in the Yucatan I would have you beheaded and your head dropped into a cenote. But this is not there. And I have other, more pressing matters. Why are you after my ammunition?"

"Why do you need so much? You've bought all of the available supply. No one else can purchase any."

"You may have a box on your way out."

Ling Fung realized he was alone in the cavern, except for dog. "One minute we fight. The next?" It was obvious dog was not going to help him figure things out. "What did they do with the team?" If he had horses, he could take the entire wagon. It was simply too heavy to push it. He took his promised box of ammunition and returned to the surface. "Wagon full of ammunition would have been good to have."

Dog did not seem to care. They rode back to Placerville.

Rip Jenkins was sitting on the porch in front of the marshal's office. "Still got that mangy hound?"

"For the moment. Woo Bo still has not found a husband."

Rip Jenkins grimaced. He pulled out his wallet, which still bore a bullet hole in the middle. "She tried to shoot me in the ass. Make sure she stays in Stockton."

Ling Fung nodded. He hoped someone would marry the girl just to keep Grandmother Woo from trying to get him to do it. He returned to his brother's house.

"Sometimes it's good to be an unsavory character." Milton Purdy sat outside.

"So sorry. Was not able to recover ammunition. It was like it was swallowed up inside the ground."

"Well, at least you tried. With no ammunition, no one wants to buy my guns. A gun's pretty darn useless without bullets." Purdy sipped some lemonade.

No one in the household ever fixed lemonade—at least not that Ling Fung could recall. "Is that lemonade?"

"Yes, your niece made some." Purdy took another sip. "Absolutely delicious."

"How would you like to go to Stockton? There's someone you should meet." It was cruel to try and fix someone up with Woo Bo, but Milton Purdy had outlasted his welcome in the eyes of Ling Fung.

He tied off his horse at the hitching post and went inside. "Lotus Blossom, where is the lemonade?"

"We don't have any."

He found the pitcher of lemonade, still half full, in the kitchen and poured himself a glass. "Mr. Purdy, I was unable to find the people who have been buying up all of your ammunition."

"That's a shame, really. They were looking forward to meeting you."

"As I suspected." Ling Fung took a sip of lemonade. "You knew all along what was happening to your ammunition."

"Big plans for California. Didn't want some annoying do-gooder getting in the way of things."

'As if I can run off to the marshal and report some guy with an owl head is going to take over the state? Do-gooder is not an apt description of me. I think you have used up my hospitality."

"Well, who was I supposed to meet in Stockton?"

"Woo Bo, nice Chinese girl. Just ask for Grandmother Woo's house. Everyone knows her." *They know Woo Bo, too,* he thought as he finished off his lemonade. They know her really well.

# 9
## SALESMEN

"Milton Purdy? That carpetbagger from Illinois?" He started to open the whisky bottle, then thought better of it. Sharp eyes and clear thinking were what Rip Jenkins needed now. Drinking heavily nearly got him married to Woo Bo. His body shuddered all over for a moment as adrenalin made him a touch jittery, but the body had to defend itself—even from a memory.

"You know him then?"

"Came through couple years ago. Said he was gonna open up some munitions factory. People were excited with the promise of so many good paying jobs. Then, the strangest thing happened." Rip paused for just a moment. "IIe just up and gets on the train and heads back to Chicago." He thought again about drinking.

"And now he returns?"

"There's something else. My counterpart, Marshal Twerp over in Stockton, just wired me. Woo Bo is heading this way."

"And you are tempted to flee before she arrives."

"She took a shot at me on the Fourth of July."

"You are wise to take flight. Where will you go?"

"Fishin' up at my favorite spot in the Sierra."

"Where is it?"

"Wouldn't be much of a secret if I went around telling folks, would it?"

"Perhaps not. But I too have a sudden urge to leave town."

"Pack your bags." He took a sip of the whisky he'd just swore off. "Be out front in ten minutes."

"Are you moving out?" Lotus Blossom asked.

"No, just a short trip."

"Too bad."

Ling Fung and dog were back in under ten minutes. And there was no sign at all of Marshal Jenkins. Or his horse. "Dog, it would seem we have been abandoned. I guess we'll simply have to find our own secret fishing place. The alternative is to stay here and see what Woo Bo is up to."

Dog barked.

"I thought as much." They headed out of town, up into the Sierra. At least it was getting warmer now. It wouldn't be quite so blasted cold. "Didn't get to pack much food. Do dogs fish?"

There was no answer from dog. He simply ran out a little farther in front of the horse.

"Perhaps you could track the marshal and we could surprise him at his camp?"

Whatever great powers and abilities dogs possessed was apparently going to remain a mystery a little while longer. Dog stopped to smell some purple flowers growing along the side of the road.

As the sun made its way lower in the afternoon sky, Ling Fung began to pay more attention to looking for a possible campsite. There was a small stream winding its way alongside the trail. The area was well protected by Ponderosa pines. "We make camp here," he told dog.

After he got the fire lit, he looked into the stream. "How can you tell if there are fish in there?"

Dog did not answer.

"Mighty Yangtze River full of fish. Ling Fung traveled on it many times. Never ate any fish from it. Never learned how to catch fish. Good thing I brought chicken to make stew."

He unpacked his bay leaves. "Good thing California have so many bay trees. Good seasoning. Add just a little bit of salt and brother has one less chicken, but we have supper."

An hour later, he scooped out a portion for dog into a cup, then took a bite himself. "Good, yes." He took a few more bites. Then he unwrapped some biscuits he grabbed from the kitchen. Brother would not be dining on chicken and biscuits this night.

"We do not have much, but we can always share," Ling Fung announced. "You do not need to hide behind tree." He held up his cooking pot. "Dog even likes my cooking. You will too."

The Yeti came out from behind the tree. Dog ran around behind Ling Fung. Ling Fung scooped out the remaining stew and placed a biscuit on top. He placed the plate on the other side of the campfire. "Good restaurant charge you thirty cents for a meal like this. You get it for free."

The Yeti slowly and cautiously came over to the fire. He picked up the plate and smelled it.

"Chicken stew. It's good. Yum yum." He pointed at dog. "Dog likes it."

Yeti took a piece of the chicken and ate it cautiously.

"So, things not work out with May Li?"

He grunted, then Yeti gulped his food down in two bites.

"Was worried that might happen. May Li doesn't seem like a stay-in-a-cave sort of woman. Have you tried to meet some nice Sasquatch gal?"

Yeti grunted.

"No luck there. How did you make it all the way from China?"

Yeti grunted again.

"I suppose Texas Rangers still looking for revenge?"

Yeti again grunted.

"Well, if I were you I'd keep heading north. Get to Canada. They say Canada is just like China."

Yeti stood. He put his empty plate down on the ground. In seconds he was gone.

"Wish you could move like that?"

Dog didn't answer. He did come around from behind Ling Fung and sniffed the empty plate.

"Well, my four-legged friend, that was most unexpected. I guess you never know what's going to turn up out here in the woods. That's why I like cities. They're more predictable."

Dog started growling. Two horses were riding up the trail.

"We are popular this evening. Perhaps they'll have shotguns. We haven't got any shotguns for gun store."

"Well, well," a tall bald man wearing an eyepatch said as he climbed off his horse. "What have we here?" The other rider remained mounted on his horse. "A Chinaman, all the way out here with his little doggie. Now ain't that cute." He looked at dog. "Careful dog, these Chinamen eat dogs."

"Was there something in particular I can help you with?" Ling Fung asked.

"We're bounty hunters," the one with the eyepatch said.

"Never would have figured that."

"Well, we're after some interesting prey." He unrolled a poster of Yeti. "Ever seen anything like this around here?"

"Certainly, we just had supper with it not more than ten minutes ago. It just crossed the creek and went off into the woods," Ling Fung said.

"Now, no need to get all sarcastic and all."

"Who would pay someone like you to pursue such a creature?"

"Government of Mexico," the man still on his horse blurted out.

The guy in the eyepatch didn't seem real happy with that news being revealed.

"Governor should get over it. Gentlemen, I have told you all I know. The creature you seek just left here." Ling Fung pointed the direction Yeti had gone.

The bounty hunters looked at each other, then mounted up and rode after Yeti. When they were far enough away, Ling Fung said, "I should have sent them in other direction." He sat next to dog. "Be glad you are a dog. Dogs know what's right. People like me are never entirely certain. Time to get some sleep."

At sunrise they broke camp and headed back toward town. About a mile down from where they'd camped they found the dead bounty hunters—each with a skull crushed by a large rock. "Never sure what to do in these situations. Jesuits say God will tell me. God never tell me anything. Well, more Winchesters. Will have to have a sale on Winchesters when we get store open." He also found a small derringer on the guy with the eyepatch. "Hmm, lady's gun. Should be easy to sell. Yeti? Well, hopefully he has gone now. Oh look, they had some jerky."

Dog barked.

"You most certainly can claim it," Ling Fung said. "Try not to gulp it down so fast. Jerky is tough meat, needs to be chewed a little." Ling Fung bit into a piece.

Dog started growling.

"Here you go. Just wanted a sample. I am amazed at the range of quality of this stuff. Some of it is barely edible. This offering is actually quite good."

Dog didn't seem to care what Ling Fung was talking about. Dog was already about halfway through the one pound pouch,

Ling Fung grabbed the pouch of jerky. "You can finish it later. Not good for you to gobble it all at once."

"Grrrr."

"You'll thank me later."

# 10
## Justice

He noticed a small trail, the sort of disruption to the forest that can go unnoticed to the untrained eye. It was an animal trail where the forest gives way to the repetitive trampling from the local animals as they go back and forth from the local watering hole to some other forest location favored for food or rest. They headed down it, trying to avoid getting smacked in the face as this was not a trail meant for a man on horseback. Dog didn't seem to be having much trouble, being much lower to the ground. Ling Fung finally dismounted and decided to go on foot. Being on foot didn't help much.

It seemed town would be closer if they could go the way they were currently going. The road seemed to take them out of the way. This deer trail headed straight for town, sort of. There was a pond right in the way. Animals liked water and had little interest in going into town.

And there was a naked man standing in the pond. He was holding a fishing rod.

"I am afraid to ask what you use for bait," Ling Fung said.

Marshal Rip Jenkins flopped around in the water until he could get out. He struggled to get into his faded pink Acme Union Suit. The fabric wanted to cling to his wet body as he tried to get dressed. "No one ever comes up here. Sorry I took off on you. Just couldn't reveal my secret spot."

"Well, I am not much of a fisherman," Ling Fung said. "We were heading back to town and decided to try this animal trail," He pointed it out. "Not recommended unless you're his height." He pointed at dog.

"That's why nobody ever finds my fishing hole. Too darn hard to get to."

As they rode back toward town. Ling Fung noticed the marshal didn't seem to have any fish. Some things were best not asked. They emerged from the thickets of vegetation and found themselves on the main road heading into town. "Over on left, who owns that ranch?"

The marshal looked it over for a few seconds. "Not rightly sure. The place belonged to George Hopper until a few months ago. Poor old George had a stroke. Not rightly sure who owns it now. We're out of town limits, this is county business out here."

"I see. Big white building might make a nice store."

"George had always said he was going to open up a restaurant, but he never did. His wife, Mabel, died from some fever around a couple of years ago, I reckon. After that, George kind of lost interest in the place."

"Interesting," Ling Fung said as he scanned the property for its potential. "And who owns the wagon and those horses in front?"

The answer came as the front door flew open and two deputy sheriffs were carrying a teenage girl out of the house. She was kicking and squirming. "Get your hands off me!"

"You boys got yourself a handful," Rip said.

"Make them let go of me!" the girl demanded.

"Miss, I know who you are. You're Megan Hopper. You're practically all grown up."

"These goons are throwing me out of my own house."

"That true boys?" Rip asked. His lawman's curiosity was starting to take hold.

"Marshal, this ain't in your jurisdiction. But we got a court order to turn her over to the foundling home."

"Foundling home? She's a little big for that."

"I'm 14," Megan said.

"And there lies the problem," the deputy explained. "Although her pappy did leave her this place in his will, she's a minor and ain't got no adult guardian."

"The county just wants to steal my land," Megan insisted.

"I see." Rip climbed off his horse.

"She's not even going to school."

"It's summer," Megan protested. Who's the Chinaman?"

"I am Ling Fung."

"Do you run that laundry in town?"

"Most assuredly, I do not. But, if we could have a moment, I have a business proposition you might be interested in."

"I ain't that kind of girl."

"No, you don't understand. This is America. People all have guns, or wish they had them." He motioned for her to follow him a little way from the crowd. They talked a few minutes, then returned. "Miss Hopper has agreed to let me rent the white building here for my new business venture. And she will work for me, at least until school starts. This will provide her with income to maintain her property here."

"Uh, congratulations, but these deputies have a court order to take her from this house," Rip pointed out. "The gist of the problem is she does not have a guardian."

"Well, while I would gladly offer, I am from a dishonest race and cannot be trusted in such matters, according to the State of California."

"Now what?" Rip asked.

So, after a little more discussion, they all found themselves at the Placer County Court House. A middle aged woman looked up from her desk, then looked at the blotter. There were no cases scheduled for that day. "May I help you?" The nameplate on her desk read *Betty Williams, Clerk of the Court.*

"Judge Green issued this here writ to remove Miss Hopper. We wanted to talk to him about it."

"Are you practicing law now, Marshal Jenkins?" The clerk asked.

"Oh no, ma'am. We just wanted to talk to the judge."

"He is not available." She thought for a moment. "What is this about?"

"Well, if we were able to get a guardian appointed for Miss Hopper, Mr. Ling here would be willing to rent part of her property, giving her some income."

"I see. That seems reasonable. Who will be the guardian, then?"

"Myself," Rip said.

"Is this acceptable to you, Miss Hopper?"

"Yes ma'am."

"Follow me." She took them into the judge's chambers. The Honorable Thurston Green was passed out on his desk. A half empty bottle of Red Eye was nearby. "He doesn't hear a lot of cases in the afternoon." She took a pre-printed form out of a drawer, then took his hand and scribbled his name on it. Then she took the court seal and stamped it. "Just fill in the full name of the guardian and that will be that."

"Do you do this often?" Rip asked.

"Well, he wouldn't remember what he signed if I didn't tell him. Or you can come back when he's sober."

"Uh, this will be fine," Rip agreed.

Ling Fung grabbed his horse and headed home. There was a letter waiting on the end table next to the door. He opened it up. "We have been selected as official dealers for the Winchester Repeating Arms Company," he told dog. "It's always Winchesters."

He noticed a second letter. This one was postmarked Stockton. "Ah, Grandmother Woo has written us."

Dog's ears picked up.

"You liked Grandmother Woo. She kept slipping you cookies. Don't act like you don't know. Anyway, Woo Bo has gotten married. Marshal Jenkins will be glad to hear that. She married that slimy Milton Purdy. He's going to build ammunition plant right there in Stockton. Nothing good can come out of that."

# 11
## GRAND OPENING

The newspaper said prizes could be won. People were lined up for the Grand Opening of Ling Fung's Firearms Emporium. Lots of people.

"There's too many of them."

"Nonsense, just people who wish to give us their money in exchange for new and used firearms." Ling Fung opened the door. "Good morning everyone. Welcome." Dog went and hid behind the counter. Megan Hopper dearly wished she'd washed her hair. There were 30 people here. She'd figured they'd do good to see one or two. It clearly paid to advertise.

They sold 17 guns that morning. Ling Fung was most pleased. And one couple still remained. Conrad Parker, Mayor of Placerville and his lovely wife, Penelope.

Penelope had eyes like emeralds. They could capture and engage nearly any man. She seemed to be talking to him, but Ling Fung was having trouble understanding her—his brain so fixated on her beauty. He didn't recall getting so mesmerized by a white woman before. Perhaps he'd been in America for too long.

Something about sheets. She wanted to know if he was moving his laundry business out here as well.

"No. The laundry belongs to my brother, Ling Ming. He is not affiliated with this store."

"That is a relief. Having to come all the way out here for my tablecloths, well that would be most unfortunate."

"Perhaps you'd like a derringer?" Ling Fung asked. "Can be concealed just about everywhere."

"Uh, charming an idea as a concealed firearm might be, the folks in town just would not understand."

"Of course." Truth was, Ling Fung detested the little pistols. They wouldn't hit the side of a barn from three feet away.

But a derringer would have been better than nothing. It was about a fifteen minute carriage ride back to town. And they hadn't used to call Placerville "Hangtown" for nothing. It had always been a violent place.

"And I get five percent?"

"Yes, Miss Hopper. That was our agreement."

❧

Sheriff Thurmond Thomas was scratching his head. He sent two deputies off to serve a writ and take some child to the foundling home in Sacramento. Every question he asked just made his head hurt. The writ had been served, but the child was still there. How was the county to seize an abandoned building that was not, by definition, abandoned? He hoped another belt of Thunderbird would clarify things. It didn't seem to.

In fact, some hysterical Mexican woman was in the office screaming in Spanish about something to do with the road out of town. "Calm down! Hank, you and Larry go out there and figure out what she's screaming about."

People get so worked up 'bout things. He leaned back in his swivel chair. If only he could stay in his office all day, but that never seemed to happen. He pulled himself out of his chair and waited for the room to stop spinning around so fast. Damned cheap whisky. It so expensive to buy Bourbon.

His horse was right where he'd left it. He almost collided with that kid reporter from the *Mountain Democrat*. Kid didn't even seem to notice him. He couldn't remember if he'd left that Mexican woman standing in his office. He sure didn't remember her leaving with the boys. Oh well, it probably didn't matter. He sure hoped she wasn't the only witness.

"His honor didn't carry a gun," somebody was saying.

"When you're that pussy whipped…"

"Well, she was a real looker. Now, with her head cut off, not so much." The speaker of those profound words was his own deputy, Hank—the reliable one. "Ah, here's the sheriff."

Thank God he decided to come out. He'd hate to see the next edition of the paper declaring local sheriff refuses to respond to grizzly triple murder.

# 12
## Riches

Ling Fung longed for an abacus. While the counting device baffled western accountants, they were a staple in Asia. Uncle Ho swore by them. But, the Jesuits had taught him western math and he was actually fairly good at it. In no time at all, he had his sales book updated and handed his land lady her cut of the proceeds. "Nothing gets people buying guns better than a grizzly unsolved murder. We have nothing left to sell."

"I'm going to get me some new shoes. I've never had new shoes before, just old ones my father found out where the transients used to camp by the railroad tracks."

It seemed like such a reasonable request. Just shoes. "Cannot advise you on women's shoes. Ling Fung buys his clothes from Hong Kong. Very good tailor there. Takes a while to get them, as they come by ship. Shoes came from San Francisco. They only have men's shoes at Hong & Ming on Sansome Street."

"Oh, in town, I know which ones I want."

Then again, why were women always talking about shoes? Even Lotus Blossom talked about them every day. Some ad in paper about shoes and, "Look father, they have shoes on sale."

"What are we going to sell now? They've bought our guns." Megan asked.

"Well, Ling Fung has ordered more from Winchester. Maybe we can find other suppliers."

"How come you don't move out here? There's plenty of room."

"Not look right. Chinese man and young white girl. No, for now Ling Fung must remain in town."

"People are such gossips. Probably wouldn't help if I charged you rent?"

"I do not think it would matter."

"Before, no one paid me no mind. Now, with all the commotion in court and the customers, they say 'Hey, there's some

**66**

helpless teenage girl all alone out there.'"

Ling Fung patted the leather pouch underneath her sweater. "Alone, yes. Helpless, no."

Megan pulled out the five-cylinder .36 caliber revolver. It used the same ammunition as the Navy Colt. It was made by Arms of Detroit, no longer in business. "I suppose."

"Dog can keep you company at night, if you wish. I do not like your being alone so far from town,"

"What's his name?"

"Who?"

"The dog. You never call him anything."

"I do not know what his name is."

"That's kind of weird. Why don't you name him something?"

"It just doesn't seem right. He is dog."

"Well, dog, wanna stay out here tonight?"

"Brrf."

She rubbed his ears. "Pappa didn't like dogs. He thought all they did was eat and poop."

"We try it a few nights." He looked at dog. "Okay with you?" It seemed to be okay. He saddled up his horse. "I'll be back tomorrow."

Time was a relative concept. To get to the house on horseback took about twenty minutes. To get there on foot took about twice that.

He could hear his brother and Lotus Blossom arguing about something upstairs. Not going anywhere near that, he headed for the kitchen. He caught himself wanting to ask dog what he wanted for supper, then remembered he was still at Megan's. She'd probably spoil him and feed him too much. He found some fried rice. It was still relatively fresh. And an onion cake. And some lemonade. This would do quite nicely. And he did not have to listen to dog snoring. Quite nicely.

And there was something about cold rice he always liked. Some people would actually throw it out. Americans were a wasteful people. But they simply left more rice for him to eat.

☯

Ling Fung was so glad he never had children—at least not any children like Lotus Blossom. She was standing in his room.

He believed it to be about two o'clock in the morning. There was no longer any noise coming from the nearby saloons. Could be even later. "Did you have a bad dream or something?"

"There's some man here to see you."

"What time is it?" he asked.

"One o'clock."

He was losing his touch. "To see me?" She seemed to have gone back to her room. Just leave the door wide open. Let in anyone who calls in the middle of the night. He staggered down to the door. "Can I help you?"

"Come with us?" a man said.

"I think not. Who are you?"

"Sheriff's office."

"What's happened?" Ling Fung asked.

"There's been a shooting involving Megan Hopper."

"Is she all right?" he asked.

"Don't know. Sheriff said to come and fetch you."

And twenty minutes later they were at her house. Sheriff Thomas and Marshal Jenkins were both there. Megan was sitting in a rocking chair on the back porch.

Ling Fung asked, "What has happened?"

Dog raced over to him.

"Your flea catcher there," the sheriff explained, "started barking. Miss Hopper found some man in the hall of her house trying to kick the dog. Well, she shot him. Fellow apparently took off. We followed a blood trial down to the creek. It ends there. We may be able to find more in the morning."

"Uh, sheriff, how did you get here?"

"Funny coincidence. I was coming back from Stockton with Deputy Reynolds. We'd picked up a prisoner. We were on the road and heard shots coming from the house here."

"Why is Marshal Jenkins here?"

"Because you talked me into being her legal guardian," he said. "Young girl being out here all by herself. What was I thinking? Megan, either you spend the nights in town or get Ling Fung here to stay out here."

"I will try living out here," Ling Fung said.

With that agreed to, the lawmen all left. Nothing was said for a while. Megan just sipped her coffee. "I shot this guy, but something else happened. I felt like something was watching me."

"Something or someone?"

"An owl. It was in my dreams, then the dog started barking." She pointed inside. "Just past the parlor is a guest room. We hardly never had guests. You can sleep there."

And so, at four o'clock in the morning, he was again trying to sleep. And he, once again, had to listen to dog snoring. Lotus blossom had won a great victory, this night.

# 13
## The Student

"Any idea what he wanted?" Ling Fung sipped his cup of coffee. "He had to have been here for a reason."

"Well, maybe he thought there was money here from your store. Maybe he just wanted to ravish me. I don't know. You break into my house you get yourself shot."

"Simple enough." He wondered how she got the pancakes so light and fluffy. The ones at his brother's house had the characteristics of concrete. One thing was certain, Megan was a very good cook.

Dog had his head in a bowl, but Ling Fung could not tell what he was eating. The animal seemed quite content.

She followed his gaze. "He woke me up. We never had a dog around. My pappy didn't like 'em."

He finished off the last drops of his coffee. "Much to do today. New shipment coming in from Winchester."

☯

Ling Fung was so engrossed logging in the new firearms that he nearly did not hear the door open. He didn't look up from his writing as he didn't want to make any mistakes in recording the serial numbers. "I will be right with you." The new customer quietly took a throwing star out of his pocket and sent it hurling at the merchant. At the last second, Ling Fung blocked the weapon with his ledger book. "Young man, you need to do more polishing. This rough a cut makes the star fly irregularly. Do better next time. And please leave now."

"Ling Fung," the assailant said in a loud and forceful voice. "I challenge you to combat."

He put down the ledger. "And why would I want to fight somebody who makes crap like this?" He pulled it from the book and dropped it in the wastebasket.

"I am a monk."

"Not from any order I've ever heard of."

"We serve and worship a living god—Ah Puch. He is from

the Yucatan, the last god of the Mayans."

"Living is one way to put it, I suppose. Go away and leave me alone."

"Our great lord has come to admire your fighting skills. He wishes to fight you," the monk explained.

"Then why are you challenging me?"

"The student must challenge first. It is the Shaolin way."

"I am not Shaolin." He knew arguing was pointless. "Tomorrow. Noon. Placerville, Main Street. Leave now." His would-be opponent bowed and left the store.

Ling Fung looked over the throwing star. He was amazed at how poor the workmanship was. He doubted his birdbrained adversary had any idea how to work metal.

"Must go to town. Can you watch store?"

Megan shrugged. "Sure."

*An Exhibition of Martial Arts!* The banner proclaimed.

"We closed the store so you can break boards?" Megan asked.

"Only way Marshal Jenkins could think of to comply with town ordinances. Fighting in public is not legal."

"I don't see why you're fighting at all."

Women never understood these things. "You women never understand these things."

Megan had dog on a leash. He was used to roaming freely and did not seem to like it.

"If you kill him I may have to run you in," the marshal warned.

Ling Fung was about to doze off. He'd slept little in his new surroundings and it was a warm day.

Megan shook his shoulder. "He's here."

His opponent was dressed in an orange robe, most likely made from silk. It looked cheaply put together. He hoped the boy would not end up naked before this event was over. Ling Fung took off his suit jacket to avoid damaging it. Suits from Hong Kong were not fighting clothes. He bowed.

His opponent—and he still did not even know the boy's name—threw a shuriken. It was as badly made as the previous one. It wobbled as it flew through the air. Ling Fung's nanchukus knocked it to the ground.

"Nanchakus," Uncle Ho had once taught him, "were good protection from flying weapons, but offered little else."

The boy moved closer. He looked barely older than Megan. Ling Fung had paid little attention to him in the store. He wanted to scold himself for his arrogance. Another throwing star was sent. Again, Ling Fung knocked it to the ground. Before any more could be thrown, he raced toward the boy and attacked him from the crane position. The boy went down. Ah Puch took a normal stance. "Your wrist is broken. You will throw no more weapons. Your master mocks you. He mocks me as well in sending you. Go back to where you are from. I do not want to see you again."

"Yes, Master Ling," the boy quietly said.

"Go by Dr. Sculls's office at the end of the street. He can send the bill to me." Ling Fung started picking up the shurikens. He wondered if he could melt them down and make a proper throwing star.

People standing around observing them started clapping. Ling Fung bowed in appreciation. It didn't take much to entertain folks.

"Thank God that's over," Megan said. "Can you teach me some of that Kung Fu?"

"Had you asked me a few days ago, I would have said no. They did not have nuns at the Shaolin Temple. However, we are not in China. And I think the more able you are to defend yourself, the better. And dog can't always be sleeping near you."

Dog looked suspiciously at Ling Fung, wondering if he was being talked about. He let out a bark to make sure no one thought he was asleep.

# 14
## The Master

"Why learn all these fighting skills when you can just pull a trigger and no more prowler?"

"Discipline. Honor. I could go on and on about these things. Look at it another way. When you run out of bullets or you can't get to a gun, a well placed kick or blow to someone's throat might be all that keeps you alive." Ling Fung sipped his tea. The tea was muddy because the water was not hot enough. Americans could not make proper tea. The alternative, coffee, was not much better.

Megan rubbed her shoulder. It hurt a lot. Ling Fung had shown little mercy when training her.

"We will let you heal a little. Take tomorrow off. Rest or do whatever you like."

"Then you can get the customer who just rode up to the store."

Ling Fung trotted over to his store. "Good afternoon. How may I help you?" He was a little surprised that his prospective customer was a woman. She seemed about his age—nice looking redhead.

"Do you sell rifles?" she asked.

"Indeed we do. I have a number of new rifles from the good people at Winchester. We also have a few used ones. Was there something in particular?"

"I need to shoot an owl."

"Most times, a shotgun is the preferred weapon for birds."

"Can't get close enough to get him with s shotgun. That's why I want a rifle."

"I see. Of course, most people consider it unlucky to shoot an owl."

"Well, this one's been unlucky since day one."

He knew he'd regret it, but he asked, "Unlucky?"

Her eyes teared up. "It's always out there, looking at us. It stays on the property of a mine they put in about six months

**73**

ago. It's like the owl owns the mine. I know that sounds crazy."

He was getting a very unpleasant feeling about this conversation. He did not know what he had done to have Ah Puch placed right smack in the middle of the road to destiny, but he could not deny it was happening. "I fear you are in grave danger."

She let out a laugh. "I already know that. Why do you think I want the rifle for?"

He took one of the new Winchesters off the rack. "This repeater is the latest thing. Have you ever fired a rifle before?"

"I'll figure it out."

He didn't like the sound of that. But he had no real reason to refuse a sale, even though he did not think this was going to turn out well.

☯

Marshal Rip Jenkins was literally shaking. Megan handed him a cup of coffee to try and settle him down. "What's wrong with you?"

"Woo Bo is in town."

"What's a Woo Bo?" she asked.

"A woman who shot the good marshal a while back." Ling Fung was amused by his total fear of this woman.

"Why don't you arrest her?"

"No, don't want to go near her."

"Relax. She just got married. I got an invitation to the wedding but did not go. Told them I had too much to do with new store opening and all."

"They didn't send me any invite." the marshal sounded hurt.

"She married that guy who's opening the munitions plant in Stockton. Milton Purdy."

The marshal turned a few shades of purple. "Why that no good snake charmer. What's she thinking marrying him?"

"At least you don't have to marry her anymore," Ling Fung pointed out.

"Yeah, I guess, considering, he can have her."

"I don't like him, either."

"Is inter-racial marriage legal in this state?"

Ling Fung nodded. "Apparently, even though we Chinese

are of a diabolical and untrustworthy nature, no one in state legislature ever got around to making it illegal to marry us. But you can't marry an Indian or a black person. But Woo Bo, she could've been your bride instead of his." He looked out the window. A buggy was rolling up. There weren't lot of them in these parts. "Oh my."

"What's wrong?" the marshal asked.

"Grandmother Woo."

"Who?"

"No, Woo."

"Woo?"

"Exactly."

## 15
## FAMILY HONOR

"Grandmother Woo, welcome to my new store." He bowed. "This is Marshal Rip Jenkins and my business partner, Megan. What brings you all the way to Placerville?"

"I fear, in my zeal to get granddaughter married, I may have her married to a very bad man."

Ling Fung nodded to Rip and Megan that he needed to be alone with Grandmother Woo. When they were outside he asked, "Milton Purdy may be involved with some bad people."

"My grandson was promised work at his new munitions factory. He was suspicious that the plant had no customers. No one has seen him since."

"There is a group of people who worship some Mayan god. They are plotting to take over California. I have encountered these people. Since I am Chinese, my testimony carries little weight here in California."

"You know of this?"

"Yes, Grandmother Woo. Milton Purdy built his munitions plant to make bullets for these people. There are no other customers. If they get their way, war is coming. And I might add there are very few troops in California. In fact, there are more navy sailors than soldiers in this state. They've even got the Negro Buffalo Soldiers patrolling Yosemite National Park. Not only is war likely, but victory cannot be assumed."

"That is most unsettling. I sometimes regret moving here from China. Nonetheless, I think the United States, with all of its flaws, would be better than serving some Mayan god." She started for the door. "I am relieved I came here."

"Relieved?" It made little sense.

"My granddaughter is a fundamentally bad person. She only cares about herself. I regret my efforts to find her a husband. She has not married well, but I still believe her husband is the one who will not prosper."

"We shall see." Ling Fung said. "I do have a plan, but it

will not be easy."

"Do whatever it takes."

"Yes, Grandmother Woo."

"Your brother has invited me to stay at his house. He said your room is available."

"I live out here now," Ling Fung agreed. "You are welcome to it."

☯

After Grandmother Woo and a very reluctant Marshal Jenkins had gone into town, Ling Fung set about preparing something for supper. He'd found some mushrooms down by the river. He hoped they were edible and weren't going to kill anyone. And fifteen minutes later mushroom soup was served.

Megan eyed it suspiciously. Dog smelled his bowl and sort of whimpered.

"Don't mind dog, there are some spices in the soup that make it kind of hot for a dog nose," Ling Fung assured her.

"Well, if I die from this, I hope it is a fast and merciful death," Megan said. She slurped up a spoonful. "This is actually not bad. And I'm still breathing. So, what's your grandmother want?"

"She's not really my grandmother."

"Well, how would I know? I'm an orphan."

"You have only been an orphan about six months. Grandmother Woo is the sort of woman who is your grandmother no matter how you are related to her. After supper, I am going to need you to gather a lot of firewood." He took a sip of soup and noticed his young business partner did not seem overjoyed with this request. "I am going to end this bird man nonsense once and for all. And an owl can see far better than I can at night. We are going to need bonfires if I am to have any chance."

She looked at him a moment. "I thought that was all over in town when you beat that guy?"

"No. Consider it a first round. Now Ah Puch will face me directly. He is supposed to walk away in disgrace as I defeated his student. But, I do not see that happening with Ah Puch."

Megan asked, "What does he look like?"

"Body of a man, head of an owl. More specifically, he tears

the man's head off and sort of burrows the bottom half of his owl body into the man's neck. This lets him take control of the human body. It is most unpleasant thing to see."

"What's in this soup?"

"There is nothing wrong with the soup. This is a real creature and I must face him. And it will be here. I certainly cannot fight something like that in town."

"You are absolutely serious. Why didn't you tell me about this before? The owl part?"

"I intended to, but never the right moment."

"I'm having trouble believing this, but you and Marshal Jenkins have been real good to me. Show me how you want your fires."

"That's the spirit."

Their tranquility was interrupted as a deputy marshal from town rode up. He seemed frantic and out of breath. "Mister Ling, you gotta come?"

"I have things I need to do here," he protested.

"Marshal Jenkins has been shot. Don't think he's gonna make it."

"Do you know who?"

"Woo Bo, that horrible woman from last year is back. She's loaded up on rice wine. Just up and shot him while he was having supper over at the café. Took three of us to get her in the jail cell. He's asking for you?"

There was certainly no way to turn down a dying man. "Well, forget the fires. We must go to town."

"I'll get the horses," she agreed.

"Know why they call me Rip?"

"No," Ling Fung answered.

"Neither do I. My momma never told me. I figured it was some fella she'd been sweet on, but never really knew. Doc says bullet's lodged next to my heart. Maybe a hot shot surgeon from San Francisco could save me. Doc Smith ain't much more than a horse doctor."

"I can hear you," the doctor protested.

"I'm a gonner, Fung."

"I wish there was something I could do."

"She said you made her marry a white man. Then she up and shot me. Always knew that woman would be the death of me."

"I made her? I hardly know her and certainly did not force her to marry anyone."

"Well. . ." And that was the end of the conversation.

Ling Fung waved the doctor over. "I believe it is customary for you to officially declare his death."

# 16
## BIRD BRAIN

It was late by farmhouse standards—probably ten o'clock at night. He'd wanted to spend the evening preparing. Instead, he spent the evening watching someone die—and die for no good reason.

"Light the fires. I'm at a disadvantage in the dark."

"How do you know anyone's even coming?" Megan asked.

"The Dutch oven is ready?"

"Yeah, it's ready. But answer my question?"

"Once challenged, I must defend that challenge. Ah Puch is so obsessed with me he can never drop the challenge he has laid down. Were we in China, after the failure of his student, he should be too disgraced to show his face here again. But he is not Chinese and we certainly are not in China. Things merely sift down to his notions of fairness. And I have no choice but to go along."

"That doesn't make any sense," Megan said.

"It does if you are me."

"Well, in case you've forgotten, I'm not you. I'm a teenage girl who sells guns to make enough money to live on. Wonder if they'll try and take my house again now that Marshal Jenkins is dead and I have no guardian."

"And I always wanted to see your country, Mister Ling," a squeaky voice came out of the darkness.

Ling Fung took his suit jacket off and folded it neatly in front of him. "I am sure China would remain quite happy if you stayed here in America."

Megan shrieked. "He really does have an owl head."

Ah Puck thumped his chest. "Recognize this body?"

"No."

"It's what's left of my student. Thought I'd put it to good use after I killed him for losing to you."

"It is my belief you wanted him to lose. If he had killed me then you could not face me here tonight."

80

"Very perceptive, Mister Ling."     Ah Puch moved closer. "No acolytes, no priests, none of my soldiers. Tonight we fight." He looked over at Megan. "This would be a nice roadside inn. I'll have Milton Purdy petition the court to be your new guardian. Maybe he can even marry you after his wife hangs. While you're off in one of my mines, I'll be relaxing here, down by the stream."

"That'll be the day."

"What a dumb ass! Milton Purdy, not you.   He just turns his business over to me, giving me all the ammunition I want. It's really worked out well.   And that wife of his, she keeps shooting people. What can I say?"

Megan adjusted the plaid blanket she was sitting on. She sort of shrugged.

"First thing, first," Ling Fung protested. "First you need to finish killing me."

"Splendid," the Mayan god of death replied. "This is going to be so much fun."

Ling Fung took a fighting stance.

"Oh, and I attack now?" Ah Puch asked.

"Not exactly." Ling Fung threw three shurikens at the same time.   The metal stars spread out into a pattern. Two of them tore into the body Ah Puch was now using.

"Little consequence. I can easily replace this body with another."

"You are a disgrace." Ling Fung declared. "Fighting is not a game. It is not for your amusement. And my throwing stars are well crafted, catching the air perfectly, unlike the mess your student tried to make."

A fourth shuriken tore into the owl part of Ah Puch. "Why didn't I see that one coming? There is something wrong with me."

Ling Fung said, "You've been given enough poison to drop an elephant."

"That's not fair." Ah Puch dropped to his knees. The owl part detached from the human body. It sort of skidded along the dirt, unable to take flight.

"Megan, now would be a good time," Ling Fung said.

Megan moved the blanket she'd been sitting on and extracted the double barrel shotgun concealed underneath. She aimed and fired. The bird shot tore into the owl. It stopped moving. "Thank you for choosing Ling Fung when you need a shotgun." She reloaded with two new shells, just in case. "Now what?"

"The kettle, my dear. We are going to cook and eat this horrible creature. Let him survive that. Ah Puch cannot be killed, my ass." Ling Fung stoked the fire. "Probably a tough like boot." He blanched the bird in the boiling water, then started peeling the feathers off.

"I hate being a party pooper, but if you poisoned him, and we eat that thing, won't that kill us?" Megan was amazed at how fast Ling Fung removed the feathers.

"There was no poison, just a harmless tranquilizer which wears off quickly. After cooking, it will be perfectly harmless."

"Oh."

Ling Fung put the owl part of Ah Puch on a spit and hung it over the coals. "Survive this. Probably will taste like an old buzzard. Nonetheless, it will be delicious." Half an hour later, he peeled a piece off with his knife. "It's ready. Tastes like shoe leather, but it's ready. Ah Puch cannot be killed. Well, he sure can be eaten."

Dog ran around behind his master.

"What's wrong with you? It's not that bad. Here, I'll cut you off some."

"Brff."

Some bushes began to shake. Then a small tree came crashing into the campground. "Well, just in time for supper."

Yeti made a loud grunt, then sat down by the fire. Ling Fung handed him a plate of roasted bird. In about two gulps, it was gone. "Why not." He simply handed the rest of the bird to the Yeti. It was gone in less than a minute. "Ah Puch cannot be killed. Ha. So, did you make it to Canada?"

Yeti grunted.

"Didn't work out? Where are you heading now?"

He grunted again.

"Marshal Jenkins got shot. Have to attend funeral or I'd go along."

The Yeti grunted again. Then, two large steps later, he

was gone.

"What was that?" Megan asked.

"Yeti, the man beast of Asia. British call him Abominable Snowman."

"Fights to the death. Owl Man. Yeti. Before I met you, my biggest worry was what to wear to the barn dance."

"Ling Fung can find somewhere else for gun store. Americans love guns. Location not matter that much."

"I didn't say you have to leave. At least I didn't have to eat that owl."

"Brff." Dog looked unhappy.

"My four-legged friend here did not get any supper. I do not think he is happy with me, either."

"Come on, dog, let's go inside and see what we can scrounge up for supper."

Ling Fung doused the fires. "Why so many people always want to kill Ling Fung? At least I'm not Marshal Jenkins. He actually got killed. Wonder if they'll have me give eulogy at funeral. Ling Fung is almost a Jesuit priest. Who am I talking to? No one here but me."

A carriage pulled off the road and stopped by the gun store. Ling Fung trotted over and opened the door. "Grandmother Woo, this is most unexpected."

They went inside the house. "I'm sure Megan can fix you some coffee."

"I cannot stay long. My driver is taking me back to Stockton. I appreciate your brother's hospitality, but I need to get home. That horrible husband of Woo Bo has returned to Chicago. He's abandoning his plans for a factory in California. I have hired a lawyer to represent Woo Bo, though I cannot imagine how he will defend her. She got drunk and shot the marshal. Now she will pay the price."

Megan poured some freshly brewed coffee. "Do you want sugar or cream?"

"This will be fine, Megan." She took a sip and nodded her approval. Then she looked at Ling Fung. "I fear your brother is a criminal. I am glad we are not really related. I think your niece is obsessed with you. You can't possibly have killed as many men as she claims"

"Thank you for your kind words."

"Well, I must be off. I have a long ride. Try not to make an ass out of yourself."

"I will, Grandmother Woo."

The carriage made it about fifty yards. Then a horrible scream filled the air. Yeti jumped on top of the carriage and threw the driver to the ground. He let out a deafening roar, which spooked the horses, making them take off at a full run with Yeti still on top of the carriage, howling.

"Like I said, I used to just worry about what to wear to the barn dance. How are you going to explain that?" Megan took a sip of coffee. "I mean, just wondering."

"Uh." He sure missed having Marshal Jenkins to talk to.

### THE END OF
### THE VENERABLE TRAVELS OF LING FUNG

# CHIN SONG PING AND THE LONG, LONG NIGHT

Laura Givens

It wasn't a bomb that stopped the ambulance, or a mine. It had been a sinkhole that had opened up thanks to a grenade hitting a frozen stretch of road. Roads constructed during war time, for the purpose of invasion, were not terribly well engineered. In defense of Tommy Chin and Fred Freeman, the ambulance drivers, that damned hole hadn't been there two hours earlier when they had first passed this way.

The German patrol that found them that day was easily as lost as Tommy and Fred. The four wounded soldiers that were the precious cargo of the busted vehicle had sustained no extra damage during the accident, but the ambulance had broken an axle and was pronounced D.O.A.

Corporal Russ Tragger had bandages over his eyes but his ear, pressed to the farmhouse door, worked just fine. "Shut up, I'm trying to hear what they're saying!" he hissed. "I ain't spoke no German since I was a kid and I can barely hear them on the radio."

The Germans had marched their American prisoners through the raging blizzard to a deserted house where they would all spend the night. Thanks to the constantly shifting battle lines no one was certain whose lines the house was behind.

Presently, Russ stepped away from the door, head slumped and was led to a dilapidated chair. "So, give." His limping sergeant whispered. "What did the kraut higher-ups have to say?"

Russ' face was stoic as he spoke, "Everyone loves a good joke and this one's a doozey." He let out a sigh that could have passed for a death rattle. Tommy Chin reached to take his pulse but was shooed away by Russ' fluttering hands. "Okay, it's like this, German intel says our guys are a few miles off from here hunkered down for the night—same for the Jerries. Come morning, if the Jerries get here first we are evacuated pronto to an SS station. They think we have some vital info and don't trust our captors out there not to fumble an interrogation."

"That makes a certain Nazi sense." Tommy shook his head.

"Oh, but you haven't heard the punch-line." Russ motioned for a cigarette and one of the wounded privates helped him light up. "If our guys, the US Army, get here first, we are to be executed so we can't spill anything and our pals in the next room are to hold them off to the last man."

Sergeant Manny Cole eased himself onto a stool. "So, if the Germans are first we get tortured and maybe killed, but if the Americans win the race we're just dead—end of story." No one spoke for some time or looked at each other in the small light of the guttering candles. At some point Private Chip Duke took a pack of cards out and started a half-hearted game of solitaire.

Finally Fred spoke up. "I don't know about any of you gents but I am not in any mood for sleep." There were grunts of affirmation from all sides. "Hey, Tommy, why don't you tell us one of them crazy stories about your Grandpa—Wingy Ding Dong, right?"

Tommy punched his shoulder. "Chin Song Ping, as you well know." He looked around the group. "No one's in the mood for crazy stories."

Corporal Russ spoke up. "Hey, just because my joke went over like a lead balloon doesn't mean we're dead yet. Whataya you say, Sarge?"

"Sure, what the hell. Maybe the Krauts will come in later with milk and cookies."

"Okay" Tommy shifted to get comfortable. "I've seen you boys looking at me like you couldn't figure out if I was colored or what. As it so happens, my Grandfather Ping was born in China. He wound up in America eventually but the first round eyed devil he ever saw—well, let me tell you the story just like he told it to me. He called this story…"

## CHIN SONG PING AND THE FISTS OF STEEL
### CHINA: 1875

The monster stood at least six-and-a-half feet tall, easily the tallest, most terrifying individual Ping had ever seen. In his mouth was a large smoldering stick, and from his nostrils smoke emerged. He was a being with deathly pale skin, glowing green eyes and flame-red hair, as wide as he was tall. Surely he must be a demon.

Ping, a mere fourteen years old, had never dreamed of such a creature as now towered over him where he lay sprawled on the busy, cobbled thoroughfare. The monster offered him a hand up.

"Dreadfully sorry, my lad, I should have been watching where I was walking." The demon spoke Chinese in a refined but odd accent.

"Oh no, great demon," Ping managed to sputter out. "It is I who must apologize for my lowly clumsiness. I did not mean to cause consternation to one such as yourself!"

The demon laughed heartily and pulled Ping to his feet. "I've been called many things in my time, lad, but never a demon. Allow me to introduce myself. Daniel O'Flay, gentleman promoter of pugilistic pageantry on three continents, at your service!" He swept off his top hat and bowed to the boy in a most courtly manner.

*Ah!* Ping thought, *an American demon.* He had heard tales of such creatures. He had also heard that such creatures were usually eccentric and rich.

"Forgive my ignorance, sir. I am called Chin Song Ping, a humble wanderer in search of gainful employment. Perhaps I may act as your guide if you are a stranger in this city. My rates are quite reasonable."

Ping was an industrious fellow and felt strongly that every man should know a trade. He had spent the past three weeks since he had left home, endeavoring to learn the trade of picking pockets. In fact, he had been trying to lift the demon's wallet when he had tripped over the American's large, booted foot. Ping seemed to possess little talent as a criminal mastermind, and saw instantly that becoming a guide to foreigners promised to be a more lucrative career path than pick-pocket.

The American scratched his whiskers. "Well, perhaps such an enterprising young man could come in handy. I'm seeking the workshop of one Ho Lai, master craftsman of clockwork wonders."

Ping straightened his tunic and smiled broadly. "Good sir, you were most fortunate to happen upon me. The den of Ho

Lai is several streets north, but you were heading south and would soon have encountered all manner of rogues."

O'Flay peered at his handmade map with puzzlement until Ping rotated the thing 180 degrees.

"Bless my soul, I do believe you're spot on there, my boy."

A bargain was struck, and Ping took charge of the man's enormous steamer trunk, previously hidden by his girth. Ping was small of stature, but the thing had wheels, and Ping was determined to be the best guide ever. He led the way through crowded, twisting streets, struggling and huffing over the cobblestones.

"Please pardon my unworthy curiosity, sir, but why has one such as yourself traveled so far from his native shores merely to have a clock made?" Ping puffed. "Are there no such craftsmen in America?"

O'Flay let out another loud laugh. "Clock? I should say not! Word is that this Ho Lai fellow has contrived a mechanical, clockwork warrior that fights better than any living man. It would make your emperor's army obsolete if such automatons were to be produced in large numbers." The man put a finger to the side of his nose and winked. "Old Ho Lai won't sell to the emperor though. He says his creation is destined for a greater purpose. I am offering him the greatest purpose imaginable … fame and wealth."

"How wonderful," Ping replied flatly as he wiped his brow and gave the trunk an extra heave.

"Ain't it though!" the American exclaimed. "By god, I mean to see this wonder of the East square off in the ring against the mighty Goliath, a steam-powered titan of my own devising! Sweet St. Patrick, but I can smell the money flowing in already."

☯

"Just how much money are we talking about?" Ho Lai had been skeptical of the scheme until the American pulled stacks of cash, local currency and greenback dollars, from his inner pockets. "My Iron Tiger is not some toy to be displayed at a yen a head."

"My good man, the beads on your abacus can't count high enough to describe the riches we stand to reap."

Ping could see a gleam in O'Flay's eyes that reminded

him of his uncle Pao when he was winning at mah-jongg. The American was on a roll.

"We'll start with a tour of your homeland, billing the match as the ultimate showdown of East and West. I'll promote the whole affair, no expense spared. I'll have every man-jack on this continent, yellow and white, convinced that his very life depends on being there to see the outcome."

Ho Lai stroked his beard so hard that Ping thought he might dislodge it. "And you say that we can do this all over the world as well?"

"Sir, in America we will tout it as the fight of 1876, the centennial slaughter! We'll wrap my Goliath in the flag and bill your boy as the Iron Menace. After that, we'll tour Europe and have tea with every blessed crowned head they've got. We, sir, will become the stuff of legends." O'Flay leaned back, smiling, and put his feet up on his steamer trunk. "That is, of course, if this mechanical man of yours is as good as you say. I look around me at these marvels you've created, and I've got to say, they all look a mite … fragile."

"Toys!" The inventor swept his hands dismissively at the mechanical birds, cats, clocks and fanciful contraptions that littered the room. "These are mere toys meant for the jaded palates of those too wealthy for their own good."

He leapt to his feet, beckoning Ping and the American to follow. They wound through rooms of obscure purpose, stocked with tools unheard of by the common man and half-built wonders that defied the imagination. Finally, they came to an enormous courtyard filled with trees that might once have been lovely but were now smashed and splintered.

In a corner there stood a statue—twelve feet tall, glittering and terrible in martial aspect. It was half-buried under shattered tree limbs. The old man rummaged in his voluminous pockets for something he seemed to have misplaced. The more he searched, the more frustrated he became, until he looked like he might rend the robes to pieces. He stopped, extricated his hands from their fruitless search, and screeched at the top of his lungs.

"Min!"

In less time than it took for Ping to look around, a young

woman emerged from a door in the wall behind the statue. She hopped nimbly over the pile of ruined wood, holding high a large brass key. Her raven hair, unfastened and wild, bounced behind her like a battle flag. She came close and bowed, offering the key to her master.

The girl took the old man's hand to guide him over the debris. He made a dismissive introduction as he took charge of the key. "This is Lee Min. She assists me in my great work. She is a woman, but that cannot be helped, I suppose. She does possess the cleverest and tiniest of hands, a useful asset in my trade."

Min smiled a roguish smile, and Ping's heart skipped several beats. She was not as pretty as the street girls he saw every night, but she had fire in her eyes and a stance that set his young libido ablaze.

He bowed deeply but never took his eyes off hers. "I am Chin Song Ping, pugilistic promoter in training, at your service."

O'Flay gave the boy a gentle wrap with his cane to remind him of his station.

Ho Lai inserted the key into the great statue and turned it with all his might. "Iron Tiger possesses not only the ability to move and fight but also the ability to think."

O'Flay laughed. "Think? Damnation man, but that is a bold claim!"

"Yes, bold but quite true. I have given him the capacity of thought by virtue of the millions of infinitesimal gears that fill his head. He also possesses hundreds of variably chaotic spring drives, allowing him to cope with any situation. Iron Tiger can plan and reason and even learn new skills." The inventor paused in turning the key to stroke the polished metal. "When wound up, he is a veritable philosopher/warrior, able to speak his thoughts as well as any man. But I assure you, he is no fragile plaything. His internal works are wrapped in several layers of raw silk and further protected by a layer of shaped bamboo and an outer shell of brass and steel. I just call him *Iron Tiger* because I like the way it sounds."

The key would turn no farther, so Ho Lai removed it and tossed it to Min. The clockmaker pressed a lever and jumped nimbly to the floor.

"I present for your most worthy consideration, Iron Tiger, the first great wonder of the modern world!"

The statue came to life in flowing motions that cleared away the surrounding fallen branches and trunks as though they were made of rice paper. Iron Tiger went through a series of movements that emulated a flesh-and-blood tiger's speed and aggressiveness. With the last of his foot movements, the metal man flicked a section of tree trunk into the air, where it was met by an enormous, gleaming black-and-red fist. The courtyard was filled with a thunderous sound as the wooden obstacle exploded into splinters and sawdust. The mechanical man bowed to his audience and spoke in a voice like a music box. "I am composing a poem on the nature of rust. Would you like to hear it?"

O'Flay whooped and tossed his hat in the air. He shook the old man's hand so hard that Ping felt sure the inventor might rattle to pieces. "Sir, let's talk turkey!"

Why they should speak of birds at this time Ping had no idea—but he didn't really care, either—as Min took him by the hands and danced around joyfully. Ping was in love.

☯

"I think I found an arm," Ping called out as he dug through straw and paper.

The warehouse was enormous and echoed with the sounds of his voice. A half-hour before, 20 heavy wooden crates had been delivered to this place that O'Flay had rented for the upcoming event. Goliath had been shipped in pieces from America, and Ping had been enlisted to assist in assembling the behemoth.

"Good lad!" the American barked. "Use that winch, and let's see how Goliath looks with both his arms."

This new career involved more physical labor than Ping cared for, but the task was an interesting one and held the promise of more dancing with the lovely Min.

"Mr. Daniel, sir, might this humble one inquire how exactly the great and wonderful Goliath will move once he is whole? Though I have seen gears and pulleys as we have assembled him, I've seen nothing of the sheer complexity we were told went into Ho Lai's Iron Tiger."

O'Flay maneuvered the arm deftly into place. "Well, I'll tell you. Goliath is a lot like me, simple but powerful. What powers him is steam."

Ping grunted as he held the arm steady to be bolted into place. "Full of steam—yes, I can see the similarity."

O'Flay eyed his assistant, then laughed. "Just so, lad, just so!"

☯

At midday, there was a knock on the warehouse door. Ping volunteered to answer it.

"Even great promoters of pugilism must eat," he said.

It was Min. She removed the wrap from a tray of turnip cakes, rice balls and a steaming assortment of vegetables. Ping had not seen its like since he left home. Indeed, it was a close thing whether he was gladder to see the food or the girl. Fortunately, they came as one package together.

"Well, bless my soul, doesn't that smell good." O'Flay came up behind him. "I suppose it is lunchtime at that, but my stomach is of a delicate disposition when it comes to local cuisine." He made a courtly bow to invite the young lady in, and Ping belatedly followed suit.

"Then this food shall go to waste, and my master will be cross." She sighed and moved toward an overturned crate.

"I should be most grateful to sample your morsels." Ping sighed.

Min tickled his chin. "I can offer only the morsels on this tray. Anything else, you should discuss with my master."

Ping turned red, and Min giggled.

O'Flay winked at the girl. "I have boiled beef and cabbage waiting for me in the back room. Why don't you two eat this, and old Ho Lai need be none the wiser." The American waddled off.

Ping filled his mouth with a rice ball as he scrounged up two smaller boxes to sit on. They ate in silence—Ping ravenously, Min less so.

Min looked at her turnip cake. "Forgive me for saying so, but you seem young to be involved with such a grand scheme."

"I'm 16!" Ping lied through a mouthful of vegetables. "I am

the fourth son of a good family." At least that was true. "I intend to make my mark on this world. I will not be like my older brothers who had their destinies handed to them on a platter of gold. I left home so that I might experience the greater world for myself."

Min nodded thoughtfully. "Ah, so your parents threw you out."

Ping almost choked on the vegetables.

"It makes no difference to me. My stepfather sought to sell me into prostitution, but Ho Lai bought me first. I was meant to be his concubine, but a man so old is rarely interested. In the end, he found me more useful as an assistant than a plaything."

Ping sat open-mouthed, then smiled. "I think we are, both of us, lucky that we have the opportunity to write what we will in our life's books." It was something his old teacher had once said to him, and it sounded wise.

They ate again in silence until the food was gone. As Min gathered dishes, Ping pulled out a stack of handbills advertising the upcoming fight.

"Yesterday, I put these up all over the city. Everywhere I went a crowd gathered and asked me questions as though I were someone worth speaking to. A week ago, I was little more than a street beggar. A month before that, I was a worthless, lay-about fourth son with no prospects whatsoever." He twirled in delight, arms flung wide. "You and I are a part of all this now. People will know our names."

Min looked at the ground. "They will know my master's name. I am merely his property."

Ping grabbed her hands. "Then I shall become rich and buy you from Ho Lai! We shall marry, and I will learn how to make mechanical men. You and your wonderfully clever hands will help me, and the world shall be at our feet."

They danced around the crates and metal body parts, and Ping wished for a time when they might do more than dance.

❧

It took the afternoon, but the steam-driven man was almost finished. Ping was ordered to bring a bucket of water. He dumped it into the boiler in the behemoth's metal back.

The American produced a large, ornate key and unlocked

his steam trunk.

"And here we have Goliath's very heart." He held up what looked to be a small log. "These are what fuel the fire. They are my own invention and are comprised of wood chips, coal, beeswax, bourbon, oil and a few secret ingredients." He tossed one to Ping for his inspection. "This will make Goliath's furnace burn like the sun itself and pressurize his steam to an unheard-of capacity. I tell you, lad, springs and fancy gadgets will be no match for the pure power of steam."

As the fire heated the water, Ping was given an oversized metal pot with slits cut into it to attach at the top of Goliath's frame. He scuttled up the hand and footholds in the side of the body.

"Sir, again I am confused," Ping said. "If this is our champion's head, where is his brain?"

The kettle attached upside-down to a hinge on the shoulders near two rows of buttons that would be under the pot when it was locked closed.

After Ping descended, O'Flay climbed up and punched the buttons seemingly at random. As he did so, a marvelous thing happened. The right arm and then the left shot out at lightning speed, powered by pistons releasing a faint hissing screech of steam. O'Flay slipped from his perch but grabbed at the hinged head to steady himself.

Goliath stepped forward, and the punches continued at uneven intervals. At the press of more buttons, the giant turned toward one of the taller packing crates and punched it full of holes. When the box was almost demolished, Goliath stepped back and raised a mechanical leg behind him. With a high-pitched sound of metal scraping metal, the foot came down and delivered a mighty kick to the crate. It flew the length of the warehouse and exploded into splinters.

Twisting a recessed valve, O'Flay released the trapped steam in a great plume and clambered down.

"Ain't he a dandy?" he asked.

Ping stood stunned. He had never witnessed such a display of sheer, raw power.

"So, you act as the brain for Goliath," Ping said. "Forgive me for saying so, but are you insane? You could never fit in that kettle and would be exposed to Iron Tiger. ... Wait one moment. You don't mean to have me be in that kettle, do you?"

Ping widened his eyes, and he felt the blood drain from his face. This career path was looking less appealing every minute.

"Hmm, you would just about fit ..."

Ping turned to flee.

The American grabbed his shirt. "I'm joking!" He roared with laughter.

Ping sighed in relief as the man went to the steamer trunk and produced a large cage. In the cage was a black rooster with a fiery comb and wicked spurs. Now Ping was truly confused.

"Meet Goliath's brain, the most vicious fighting gamecock in all Vinegaroon country, Texas." He poked a finger at the bird and almost got it snapped off for his effort. "I got the idea at an Indiana carnival where a fellow had taught a chicken to add up totals by pecking on the keys of a cash register. This is the same principal. This noble fowl has incredible fighting skills bred right into him, so all I had to do was teach him to express his talent for mayhem by pecking at the buttons that control our ferrous gladiator. I can't put him in right now without an opponent to strike at. Lord only knows what he'd do. But I assure you he will be hell and hotspurs when the time is right."

Gingerly, O'Flay returned the rooster to the trunk. "Don't just stand there, my boy. We have leaks to be sealed and lots of oiling ahead of us if we're to be ready to take on that giant celestial windup toy next weekend."

As Ping hauled away empty packing crates, he thought of something else his old teacher had once said. The old man had yelled it at him—many years ago—when he had been caught in the act of drawing pictures on a priceless scroll. Something about Ping living in interesting times, but he had shouted it as though it were a curse. This was a time much more interesting than anything that had ever happened back home, and it was most enjoyable! Crazy old man. He shouldn't have left the scroll lying around like that.

☯

Ten days had transformed the warehouse into something fabulous. Rows and rows of long steps had been erected for people to sit on, and everything was draped in brightly colored paper. Torches and lanterns transformed the cavernous edifice to noontime brilliance. It was a very large space, but the excited crowds threatened to fill it to bursting.

For two weeks, urchins on every street corner had been given rice in return for shouting about the fight of the millennium. Colorful handbills covered every square inch of every public wall. Prostitutes were paid to whisper in their client's ears as they slept about how they must see this once-in-a-lifetime battle. No betting parlor was without long odds one way or the other on the fight's outcome. People wagered their life's savings on which contender would emerge triumphant. This was the crowning jewel in Daniel O'Flay's promotional career.

"What the hell do you mean, the rooster doesn't feel like fighting?" O'Flay yelled at Ping as he coaxed the gamecock into the steel head.

"I think, perhaps, the crowd has dampened his enthusiasm," Ping replied. He poked the bird.

"Well, do something! This crowd didn't pay to see a tea dance! They will burn us alive if we don't give them their clash of titans!"

Ping made a despairing face and bowed to the rooster. "Oh fierce and mighty brain of the great Goliath, please forgive this worthless one for what he must now do."

He grabbed a couple of tail feathers and yanked as hard as he could. Ping almost lost an eye and half his face before managing to slam the kettle shut. He leapt to the ground.

"I believe I have managed to sufficiently motivate the bird brain," he reported to O'Flay.

"Excellent! Prepare the boiler."

The American grabbed a huge megaphone and sprinted to the center of the marked-off arena.

Ping jammed in the log. The gauges climbed. Across the room, Min labored at the final key turns for Iron Tiger. Her hair was elegantly styled, and she wore rich robes of bright colors. Ping sighed. This was a wonderful career he had stumbled into.

Ho Lai met O'Flay in the center, and each delivered a prepared speech, simultaneous with the other, in his native tongue through oversized megaphones.

"Gentlemen! Countrymen!"

The crowd quieted to a buzz.

"You are here today to witness a battle unlike any other in the history of the world." The crowd exploded in cheers. "You have the privilege tonight to see the dawning of a new age, an age where machines clash in a way that, before tonight, only men were thought capable of.

"These two mighty gladiators will vie for the privilege of destroying each other for your amusement and gratification. Let the battle begin!"

The entrepreneur and the inventor each ran for cover as their assistants hit the respective mechanisms that would unleash the energy embodied in their engines of destruction.

Goliath barreled forward like a runaway locomotive, while Iron Tiger swept ahead like a god of death, dancing to meet his victim. Each stopped short of contact, choosing instead to circle, watching for a weakness or a chance opening.

Iron Tiger struck first, going low to sweep an enormous leg into his opponent, seeking to unbalance him and even knock him over. Despite Goliath's enormous bulk, his own legs bent in a piston-fast motion and propelled him upward several feet when he straightened them. This allowed Iron Tiger's leg to pass harmlessly under the steam man's bulk.

The entire structure shook when Goliath landed. Onlookers fell off their seats, and people rushed to save the tinder-dry building from overturned torches. The audience went wild! This was the grand spectacle they had been promised.

Iron Tiger recovered and punched Goliath's side, spinning him twice around. When faced in the right direction once more, Goliath closed in and delivered a thunderstorm of piston-powered blows to Iron Tiger's midsection. Echoes from the blows drowned out even the crowd's hysterics.

An open-handed downward chop to Goliath's head left a huge dent in the kettle but served only to infuriate the chicken within. The fowl tried for a punishing uppercut but Iron Tiger rolled over backward in a smooth motion to escape the sledgehammer blows. Goliath chugged forward to continue his assault, but Iron Tiger had cart-wheeled around Goliath's flank, which allowed him access to the boiler in the back. Hard as he tried, Iron Tiger could not penetrate the rolled sheet metal body, so he kicked behind Goliath's knee.

Somehow the wily gamecock anticipated the move and bent Goliath's knee just in time to trap Iron Tiger's foot. Iron Tiger hopped on one foot as Goliath sought to crush the captured foot in his knee joint. This death dance lasted for another minute until Iron Tiger dislodged himself by falling down and using his free foot to extricate its mate.

Goliath turned in place but found his opponent had rolled away and regained his footing. Again they circled, offering feints and half-hearted kicks. Iron Tiger bent back till he was balanced on his hands then shot his legs under Goliath's arms, lifting him off the ground. The steam-powered leviathan flailed helplessly as Iron Tiger flung him toward the cheering crowd. The metal giant wound up landing on his back but used his momentum to roll to his feet, a move few would have thought possible for one of his size. The metal shell which encased Goliath's brain intensified his outraged squawks to something resembling a war-cry as the behemoth strode back into the fray.

Iron Tiger released his hands from their wrists where they dangled on strong cords. He quickly set them into deadly motion, swinging them at his sides like twin maces. The detached fists drummed on metal man like a chorus of gongs.

Goliath, in turn, let his left arm drop in a pendulum motion and continued the arc behind his back and up over his head, extending an extra foot as it did so. The blow came down squarely on Iron Tiger's head. A clang shook the rafters.

A hush fell over the crowd as the head of the Chinese champion cracked open on one side. Small gears went flying and left an exposed spring-wire vibrating from the blow. Tattered silk hung off shards of shattered bamboo.

Iron Tiger twitched in jerky spasms as his hands retracted back into his arms. Sensing victory, Goliath closed. With a sudden, unexpected burst of speed, Iron Tiger met him with a spinning kick that sent the kettle head and fowl brain flying from great metal shoulders, tumbling unceremoniously to the ground. Goliath froze in mid-stride as his twitching counterpart danced an epileptic jig toward the scrambling gamecock. There was a defiant crowing and brandishing of heel spurs, cut short by the crunch of a brass boot grinding into sand. The fight looked to be ended in a puddle of blood and feathers.

The audience was beside itself with emotion. The clapping, whistling and cheering bounced off the distant walls. Some cried, some danced and others exchanged large sums of money.

Then, above it all, came a harsh yet musical voice. It was the sound of an insane calliope, and it issued from Iron Tiger's battered face. "I need my key, I must be free!"

A hush came over the arena as the mechanical man gyrated wildly toward Min and his aged inventor. Ho Lai ran to meet his creation with consoling words and promises that he would never use his poor Iron Tiger thusly again. Iron Tiger picked up the old man in both hands and ripped him in two, sending the halves flying into the audience in scarlet streamers. His gaze returned to the girl, and he resumed his crazed dance forward.

"I need my key! I must be free!"

Panic reigned as several thousand patrons tried to flee the carnage.

Ping and O'Flay ran at the insane artificial man, but too late. Iron Tiger took the outstretched key from Min's trembling hand and casually backhanded her. Her broken form went flying several yards to where she landed on the dirt floor.

Iron Tiger turned and plucked a loose gear from his head. With one swift, graceful motion, he flung the gear, sending it deep into O'Flay's neck. Blood gurgled from the American's mouth and jugular. He staggered another step before collapsing in a well-dressed heap.

Ping barely managed to dodge a killing blow by diving between the monster's legs. The boy threw himself atop Min's still form and waited for a final strike.

Iron Tiger, however, had already lost interest in them as he stalked toward the fleeing hordes. Once again, the mad calliope voice cut through the din. "Where are you going? You haven't heard my poem about rust yet!"

Min's eyes fluttered, and Ping bent close to hear.

"Please," she whispered. "Do not let this slaughter be how my master is remembered." She breathed out one last time, and Ping smelled rose petals and honey.

How could a death this ugly smell so sweet? A tear fell onto her rigid cheek, and Ping felt more helpless than he ever had.

He looked and saw Iron Tiger crushing hapless audience members as he recited his poem. He also saw the unmoving form of Goliath, still poised for battle, and an idea formed in the back of his mind. He could see that it was a stupid idea almost immediately, but, as no other presented itself, he decided it would have to do.

Iron Tiger held a patron aloft by his throat so that the man might better appreciate the nuances of his verse. That the man was dead seemed not to concern the automaton at all. "Red and gritty thou art, and the destroyer of all that gleams. The very air conspires with you to …"

A voice from a large megaphone broke Iron Tiger's concentration. He turned to see who might dare interrupt his poetic masterpiece.

It was Goliath with a small, four-limbed pimple on his shoulders instead of a head.

"Come back and face me, mighty warrior." Ping hollered through the open-ended cone. "We still have matters between us and, besides, your poetry is quite terrible!" He threw aside the megaphone and pressed buttons until Goliath lumbered forward.

Iron Tiger ripped the head off the man he held before him. In one swift, fluid motion he was back in the arena, crouched in a fighting stance. Ping hit the punching buttons as fast as he could and barreled straight ahead.

Ping had never considered himself much of a fighter, and with good reason, but this attack seemed his best bet. He had to buy time while the steam in Goliath's body built to critical.

Iron Tiger bounded across the floor, arms flailing in savage lunges that would rip his foe to pieces. They met in a great clash and clanging of metal that almost sent Ping flying from his perch. Punches rained down on each other's bodies, neither able to topple the other.

Ping's legs were wrapped around what was left of the kettle latch, his hands free to hit buttons. Finally, above the screams of terror, above the sound of metal hammering metal, he heard the slight squeal of escaping steam and knew it was time.

He shifted Goliath's stance to straight up and let loose a haymaker to Iron Tiger's head. Enraged, Iron Tiger took a wild swing at Ping himself but missed when Goliath ducked into a low crouching position.

Ping rolled off Goliath's shoulders and hit a lever. All the pent-up steam power was released at once into the leg pistons to power one enormous jump. Goliath shot up through the roof in a cloud of expended water vapor.

Seconds later, the steam dissipated, leaving the fourteen-year-old boy sprawled on his backside, facing the unstoppable, clockwork monster. He scuttled back, forcing Iron Tiger to step closer. The metal man raised his foot above Ping and held up the key to show his triumph.

"I have my key and now I am fr   "

He was cut off by a high-pitched whistling sound. Ping rolled madly away as Goliath's metal body plunged back through the hole in the roof it had made seconds before.

In that instant, before the wonder of the East was crushed by the hurtling Goliath, Ping thought that he saw a puzzled look come over the rigid metal face of the mighty Iron Tiger— but perhaps it was only a trick of the light. The collision sent off a shockwave that knocked over anyone unlucky enough to still be in the building. Then, literally, it brought down the house.

☯

The next day, the authorities searched through the rubble, rescuing survivors. Chunks of twisted brass and steel were found a mile away. Those responsible were thought to be dead, victims of their own greed and hubris.

But Ping had managed to evade the falling debris and angry officials who sought someone to blame this all on. Fearful that he might be recognized, he stowed away on the first conveyance leaving the city that presented itself: a hog wagon bound for parts unknown. That suited Ping just fine.

His heart was heavy as he turned to a porcine companion who seemed to be an especially good listener. "I am an utter failure as a pugilistic promoter—no, it's true—and I failed Min as well." He rubbed away snot and tears with his sleeve.

"Surely there is something, someone in this world, even for one such as me, but I can't see it at the moment."

The swine grunted and rutted in the muddy wagon.

"Yes, perhaps you're right. Maybe tomorrow will be less interesting." Ping snuggled in next to the hog for warmth and watched the sun as it slowly set.

Private Winston whistled softly. "Holy shit, I think I read about that fight once in Ripley's Believe it or Not—but there wasn't anything about chickens or poetry."

Tommy raised his hands in supplication. "Now that's just the exact way Grandfather Ping told it to us kids. Mama always said that he was kind of fast and loose with things like facts."

The sergeant smiled and shook his head, "And I always thought my old man could stack it high. He lit another candle from one that was ready to sputter out. "So did Ping take the first ship to America to find fame and fortune?"

"No Sarge," Tommy stretched "He hung around China for a few more years. He wanted to make something of himself, as long as it didn't require hard work." Everyone chuckled, "Why, I probably never would have been born if he hadn't run afoul of "circumstances"—that's what he always called it when he screwed up.

Ping never did anything by half measures and when he hit the states he found plenty of "circumstances". He also found my Grandmother, Louise...but I'm getting ahead of myself. He always referred to this story as...

## CHIN SONG PING AND THE FIFTY-THREE THIEVES
### THE AMERICAN SOUTHWEST: 1881

As near as he could figure, Ping had fallen into one of the levels of hell. The sun stripped all color from the barren landscape. The mind-squelching heat seemed to assault him from below and above equally. The horizon stretched farther than he would have thought imaginable only a year before, and there was no relief in sight. This level of hell had a name, and the name was Arizona.

He wasn't terribly surprised at being in hell. His mother had always said it was where he would wind up, after all. What he did resent, though, was *walking* through this place of damnation while leading a magnificent white stallion that refused to be ridden.

For the eighth time that day, he stopped and bowed to the stallion. "Great and honorable steed," he said. "I realize you are far too noble to be ridden by a scoundrel such as my humble self, but we may move out of this place much faster on your four feet than on our six collective feet." He bowed lower and added, "Please?"

Ping clambered into the saddle resting on the broad, white back of the animal. He did all the "giddyup" things he had seen white riders do, to no avail. For the eighth time he slid to the ground, thinking that the problem was speaking Chinese to an American horse. He was naturally good with languages and understood English well enough, if it was spoken clearly, but the best he could manage to remember right then was, "Horse, go now, please!" and that had just seemed to irritate the animal.

So he walked, heading southeast for no particular reason other than that it was away from the railroad.

It had begun a year ago, when his all-too-brief career as an acrobat ended badly following private instruction in contortion from the wife of the head acrobat. He decided that women and his handsome face were a formula for failure. So he became a gambler—a very male-oriented profession, indeed. After an early run of good luck, he had the bad luck of continuing his winning streak in a game of chance with several brothers in the local Tong. An upturned table, an escape through a window and a daring chase across the city's rooftops had led to him blending in with a group of men gathered at the docks. He subsequently found himself herded onto a ship headed for America. He was to become a railroad worker. He wasn't sure what, exactly, that meant, but it was a career he had not tried before.

Being a Chinese worker for the Central Pacific Railroad was back-breaking, demeaning and boring work, so he again took to gambling most nights, just to keep his skills fresh. At first, he gambled only with other Chinese, but they had very little money. So as soon as he learned enough English, he sat in on poker games with the Americans. It was another bad career move. Drawing four aces to Chauncey O'Donnell's three kings had put him on the work-gang foreman's permanent bad side—so much so that Ping had found himself in the basket three days later, when blasting into a hillside was required a unique method of planting explosives had been developed by the Central Pacific.

You lower a Chinese worker over the cliff side in a basket to set the explosive and light the fuse, and then you haul him up as quickly as possible. Often, the man even survived. Ping kept his eyes closed during the descent and quickly planted the charge and lit the fuse. He screamed to be pulled up and was raised a couple of yards before his ascent stopped. He hollered and looked up to see the smiling face of Mr. Chauncey O'Donnell. "Looks like you ain't so lucky today, China boy!"

Stunned, Ping reached down to snatch the fuse, but he was too far away. Laughter wafted from above. He started his basket swinging while keeping a close eye on the sizzling fuse. As it reached its last sputter, he leaped from the basket at its highest arc, tucking into a ball and rolling with the blast as it sent him high into the air. At the moment he felt himself begin his downward plummet, he went spread eagle in an attempt to impede his fall. He landed square on the head engineer's large, snowy-white tent.

Extricating himself from yards and yards of canvas and cursing white men, Ping sensed that this might be the time for another career shift. Perhaps horse thief. He grabbed the large water skin hanging off a post and leaped onto the engineer's beautiful white stallion. He'd never ridden such a beast before, but the situation provided the necessary learning incentive. He took off like a shot. Random gunfire and angry yells receded as he urged his stolen steed in the direction that he had seen whites point toward and call Arizona.

☯

Deep in a cavern, in the mountains southeast of Tucson, a man with sly features and ancient eyes danced. He danced not in any particular step known to the feet of man but a mad dervish of joy and self-congratulation. He giggled at his own cleverness as he danced.

Behind him were four cages of a size and strength to hold a human being. The two cages in the middle held two young women who sat in despair, one black and the other Oriental.

Though clothed in elegant attire, all hope had fled their expressions, and tracks of tears, long spilled, streaked their lovely cheeks. To the side of the cells was a natural hot spring, large enough to bathe in. It bubbled and hissed sulfurous odors, and an unnatural glow shown from deep within. Louise, the young black woman, spat vehemently at the pool.

"Why don't you just get this over with, Moses? At least then I wouldn't have to watch you try to dance, you crazy ol' dog," she hollered.

The sharp-featured man stopped in mid-gyration and ran to Louise's prison. "Don't pout so, my Nubian beauty," he purred. "Your time will come, and there's always the chance the baron will come through with your ransom." He sighed. "Now, that would be a pity. This is working out so well."

He snaked his nervous hand through the bars to touch the hem of her dress. Louise kicked at him. He withdrew and licked his fingertips like he was finishing a Sunday chicken dinner.

"I swear I can just taste the power inside you." His eyes rolled up in their sockets in pure ecstasy. "Today, however, our celestial princess shall be the star attraction." He nodded toward the other cage, where the young Oriental woman sat dejectedly. "A pity she refused the opium though." The girl whimpered slightly.

"I hope you aren't so foolish when your time comes, dear Louise. I do so hate to see a dumb animal suffer." With that, he jumped across the bubbling stone cauldron and shouted, "So much to do, our guests will arrive any moment now!"

Red light filled the cavern, casting weird shadows wherever Moses Castle danced. Sometimes the shadows were of a man, sometimes of a dog. Some of the shadows bore no resemblance to anything found outside a nightmare.

Louise reached through the bars of her cage to May Song, the girl in the next cage. "We still here, and we still got a chance," she said soothingly. "My mamma used to tell me stories about princesses who was in lots worse jams than this." May Song gripped her hand tightly. "They's always a hero in them stories somewhere. He's coming, we just got to hang on till he does." She smiled tightly. This wasn't a fairy tale, and she knew there weren't any heroes in real life.

At least it wasn't flat. After a night's march farther, Ping had finally come to the boulders scattered around the foothills of a mountain range that stretched to the north. He saw a cloud of dust approaching from the east and was unsure of what course of action he should take. In desperation, he thought to consult his traveling companion.

"Great and honorable steed," he said, bowing, "there are many men coming our way. They may be our salvation, or they may be our doom." The horse nodded. "They come from the wrong direction to be those who might chase us, but there is the mystery of the telegraph, which could have foretold our coming. They might also be those known as Apaches. I am told they have no sense humor in these matters." He wrinkled his brow. "Of course, any random band of white men might also find distraction in disposing of me and acquiring you."

The horse lowered his head and shook it distractedly. "Yes, you are wise, oh noble one. Let's hide!"

Soon he and the horse were concealed behind a boulder. Ping peered through the heavy brush.

The dust cloud soon became a large group of hard-looking white men led by three men with dangerous expressions and red sashes around their waists. When they came to a rock face near where Ping lay hidden, they sat to let the dust settle. Then the three leaders wailed loudly, like amorous wolves or coyotes on a moonlit night. The ground beneath Ping rumbled as the rock face pivoted upward with a frightening majesty that froze most of the riders and frightened their horses.

When the way was completely open, the men with sashes swore and gestured wildly to move them all into the cave. Once the rest of the group had vanished into the hillside, the three whooped, shot off their pistols and galloped after the others.

As the stone slid slowly back into place, Ping sat wide-eyed and slack-jawed for a few heartbeats. America was such a strange place, and Arizona doubly so. However, as odd as what he had just seen was, what he smelled was opportunity.

He bowed briefly to his steed and said, "Stay!"

Ping ran around the boulder, legs pumping in a way that might have prolonged his short career as a messenger many years ago. He dove for the diminishing opening, tucked into a roll and propelled himself into the dark interior which, he belatedly admitted to himself, had all the makings of a fine tomb.

He stayed in a crouch as his eyesight adjusted to the gloom. He was alone.

But somewhere farther down in the Earth's bowels came a grumbling of loud, masculine conversation. A faint reddish glow made his surroundings even more surreal. The smell of opportunity had been replaced with the unpleasant whiff of sulfur. He glanced back at the now-closed stone wall. He took a deep breath and moved forward in a cautious, but determined, trot.

It wasn't a straight course. Several times, he thought he was surely lost, but then a snatch of echoed conversation or scratches of hooves on the floor steered him back onto the correct path. Finally, he came to the entrance of the main hall where the voices were loudest. He was about to peek around the entryway when a man's hat brim came into view, followed by a long arc of tobacco spit.

Ping thought retreat was a wise tactic, so he backed away quickly and silently until he tumbled down a short flight of roughly carved stairs into a smaller chamber. He dusted himself off and made sure his bones were sufficiently intact. In this chamber, the red glow had taken on a more golden hue. Slowly, he perceived the room was filled with stacks of paper and piles of things that sparkled or glowed with a warm luster.

Gold, jewels, American money. He lost no time in stripping off his shirt. With the practiced movements of a one-time escape artist, he tied off the sleeves and neck openings with strong knots and filled it until he thought sure the seams would split. Finding quality garments was difficult on a railroad worker's salary.

Ping smiled broadly and was about to make a hasty escape when, through a ventilation hole in the wall, he heard a woman cry out in fear and anguish. He stood and glared at the ceiling, reciting under his breath all the reasons he should keep going. He was a career thief now, and he had to learn to harden himself to his more tender impulses.

Then there was another scream and a woman's voice

pleading for help, in Chinese. This was followed by loud, coarse laughter and jeering whistles.

Okay, one look wouldn't hurt. He dropped his loot and scrambled up a massive pile of gold and into the ventilation hole. A series of twists and turns brought him to a wooden-grated opening that overlooked an enormous cavern and four cages.

☯

Moses Castle stood on a platform, resplendent in a crimson robe, and faced a room full of trail-hardened men. He dangled the young Asian woman over a steaming, water-filled pit as his audience of desperadoes whistled and cheered. The girl's wrists were bound, held high by only the robed man's strong right hand. Every few seconds, he dipped her low enough for the bubbling water to scald her feet, causing her to scream. The men hooted their approval every time.

"I am Moses Castle and, like that Moses long ago, I will deliver you into the Promised Land!" he shouted.

The crowd went wild.

"You have been chosen to carry out my law in this land, and my law is chaos and violence! You will do this, not for my pleasure but because it is your pleasure!"

More cheers and hooted laughter rang off the cavern walls.

"You fifty men will wear the red sashes that will make you my special brand of cowboys, and you will be invincible from this day forward. That invincibility does not come cheaply though, it requires sacrifice."

Moses frowned, then threw his head back in a loud laugh. "Not a sacrifice by you, my friends, but *for* you!"

He turned to the young woman whose life he held so literally in his hand. "A shame to waste one so lovely on such a pack of mangy curs, but it's for a worthy cause," he crooned in flawless Chinese, a glint in his eye. May screamed as loud as she could.

A long gleaming knife appeared from nowhere in Moses' left hand. With a movement as quick and devious as his features, he cut the woman's delicate throat, sending a streamer of blood across his audience. Then, with a flourish, he let go of her bound hands. She dropped into the pit. Water splashed over the sides in a hissing tide of deep red as she disappeared into her churning, watery grave.

Eerily, a searing red light erupted from the water's depths and cast Moses' shadow in stark relief on the far wall. It was no human shadow but that of some great beast howling at an unseen moon.

As the commotion in the audience slowly died down, Moses produced an armload of virgin-white strips of silky cloth. He dipped each one into the bloody pool until it came out soaked, dripping red, like a bandage used once too often. These he handed to the three men who already wore such sashes.

Like deacons, the three moved through the throng offering an unholy baptism to their congregation. At each new initiate, a soaking red sash was wrung over the man's head, then tied around his waist with the snarled word, "Brother." After all the men had been so anointed, Moses ascended his platform and let out a mournful wail to recapture their attention.

"Boys," he drawled, in a decidedly less formal tone, "You're cowboys now, and that means you step aside for no man. If you want it, you take it! No one can hurt you. You can laugh at bullets and eat knives for breakfast, as long as you wear those sashes."

Several men looked at their waists with dubious expressions. "Oh ye of little faith!" Moses shouted with glee. He pulled a .45 Colt from his robe and shot the man nearest to him. The owl-hoot looked frantically at his chest for a wound, but there was nothing but a small hole in his shirt. Wide-eyed with delight, he joined Moses and the throng in a good laugh.

Soon, men were shooting one another and generally having themselves a good old time. The walls echoed with thunder and mad laughter.

After a while, Moses set his feral features into a mirthless grimace and howled once more for silence.

"With you men, we are now 150 strong, and we will keep growing. We are going to be a god-damned army!" No longer able to contain his joy, Moses jumped up and down, whirling as he did. "Now get the hell out of here," he screamed, "and don't let me be hearing anything good about you. You got that?!"

The cowboys ran to their horses, tied along posts at the

rear of the cavern. They laughed and punched one another's shoulders until the last men were saddled up. As one, they rode into the stone maze that would lead them to the outside world—and glory. The clattering echo of hooves mingled with yelling and the rumble of stone grinding on stone until the cacophony receded into silence.

Moses could barely contain his sense of self-satisfaction. He wished that there were two of him so he could shake his own hand and pat his own back. Instead, he settled for dancing around the cave. When his revels brought him close to Louise's cage, he stopped dead in his tracks and sat on the stone floor.

Moses turned to Louise sitting stolidly in her lonely cell. "Cry havoc, my dear, for I have just unleashed the dogs of war."

Louise sneered through fresh tears.

"What must you think of me?" He sighed. "You've watched me kill three women so that I could give power to men not worthy to stroke your cheek."

Louise looked him straight in the eye. "I ain't afraid of you. You just some crazy man likes to watch folks suffer. I seen your kind when I was a girl—night riders with torches and masks. I see through your mask!"

Moses clutched his hands to his heart. "Girl, you wound me deeply! Can you not see the enormity of my plan? Each of you lovely creatures was chosen with great care, stolen away from your destiny with infinite guile and cunning. A recipe this big requires only the best ingredients." He leapt into the air, clicked his heels together and held up a single finger.

"Let's see, there was Susan Bright Water, snatched right from her wedding bed—the unconsummated bride of the Sasquatch chief himself. Can't go wrong stealing from Sasquatch." He giggled. Gloating was half the fun.

A second finger joined the first. "Lady Carmady, plucked at the height of ripeness, fresh from a holiday in the haunted woods outside Salem. I wonder if her coven is still looking for her."

Louise shook her head. "That girl today, May Lee, she weren't nothing special. She was just a mail-order bride for some big shot owns a telegraph company. Why'd you have to go and kill her?"

Moses pushed his face to the bars of the cage, screaming gleefully at the top of his lungs. "Because I hate telegraphs!"

Several deep breaths cleared the madness from his eyes so he could continue. "What place is there for mystery and magic when just anyone can speak to anyone else over such distances? Those wires strangle every bit of the romance this land once knew." He wiped drool from his lips. "Besides, she is a seventh daughter of a seventh daughter, and those are always magical. You, though, my dear, are my crown jewel. When I sacrifice you, it's going to be quite the soirée. Your grandmother was hot stuff in her day but she's gone. Marie Laveau is dead, and everyone is going crazy looking for little Louise Laveau, but I've got you! You are mine, mine, mine!"

Louise rolled her eyes in disgust. "I keep tellin' you I ain't got no special powers. I don't know no voodoo hoodoo."

Castle looked ready to split a gut, he was so happy. "Baron Samedi says he'll pay handsomely for your return—but I never liked that skull-faced bastard, so I think I'll just stick to plan A!"

Just then, they heard the faint echo of a howl and felt the grinding tremble of the great stone door opening and closing.

"What the hell did those idiots forget this time?" Moses listened for the sound of hoofbeats, but none came. "That's peculiar."

He scratched his neck as he went to the middle of the room, cocking his head to listen. Nothing!

As he turned back to the cages, he heard a pop. A flash of light exploded in the middle of the chamber's doorway, leaving a thin veil of smoke. Then a second and a third until the entire doorway was a thick, hazy curtain of vapors. Through this curtain strode a short, young oriental man with strong, handsome features. He was wrapped from head to toe in a loose toga of fine heavy silk. His wavy black hair flowed around his shoulders. The newcomer's face was split from ear to ear by a warm infectious smile as he bowed low before his robed host.

Moses snarled in perfect Chinese, "Who the hell are you, and what the hell do you want?"

☯

Ping had watched in horror, through the wicker ventilation grid, as the man in robes slit the young woman's throat. He could not hold back the anguished cry of anger and frustration that exploded from his lips.

That might have been Ping's undoing, except that he was entirely drowned out by the general pandemonium that reigned on the cavern floor.

The only person who heard him was the young black woman trapped in the cage below him. Her head snapped up toward Ping, and their eyes locked. Hers were the most wonderful eyes Ping had ever beheld, dark and gleaming with sudden hope. She was darker than any woman he had ever known. The red luminosity from the pit gave her an aura of sensuality he had never imagined. He fell in love immediately. This was terrible timing for one looking to start a career as a hardened criminal.

He put his finger to his lips then motioned that she shouldn't look at him, but they couldn't keep their eyes off each other.

He mouthed, "My name is Ping."

She returned, "I'm Louise."

Louise. That was such a wonderful and exotic name.

Out in the cavern, a strange and unholy ceremony was being performed, but all of Ping's thoughts were focused on those large, luminous brown eyes.

His mind raced. He had been the student of one of China's great escape artists, so he ought to be able to pull off a simple rescue/escape. True, his master had let him go when he proved to be inept at picking pockets while the great man was performing, but he had learned much in that month and a half.

He ran through his options.

He could smash through the grill, leap onto the cages, climb over to the prison of his new beloved and ... be cut down by a room of madmen. Terrible escape plan.

On the other hand he could ... what?

When the shooting started, Ping was snapped from his reverie. Plans were overrated anyway, he thought. He would figure out something. With a final blown kiss to Louise, he crawled backward through the ventilation shaft. With no room to turn around, he fell back into the treasure chamber, where he tumbled down the mound of gold to land lightly on his feet.

He grabbed his improvised sack and was almost out the door when he spied a roll of intricately printed silk propped against a wall. In a flash of inspiration, he grabbed the richly woven cloth and bounded up the stairs three at a time. It wasn't a plan exactly, but it was a start.

As he sprinted back the way he had entered, he tried desperately to remember the correct turns. He soon came to the dead end that marked the cave's entrance. Spinning around like a top, he spied a dark alcove he had failed to notice earlier and lunged into its scant protection.

His back pressed against the cold stone. He stashed his stolen booty at his feet. The cleft in the rock provided some semblance of shadows, so Ping closed his eyes, breathed deeply and willed himself to be as insignificant as possible. He listened to the echoes of gunshots, trying to recall his brief training as an actor.

"Be the rock, be the shadow, be invisible," he whispered.

After what seemed an eternity, he heard the rumble of riders and horses. Eyes squeezed tighter, he said a silent prayer. The sound was almost upon him. Over the din of hooves, hammering on solid stone, fifty-three voices were raised in a howl of sheer, murderous delight. Ping's knees felt wobbly. The wall trembled against his bare back as the great stone rose.

He thought he might soil his only pair of pants.

The din eventually died down until there was only the grind of stone on stone. He risked opening one eye.

The door was more than half-closed, with no sign of the horsemen. Pretending to be invisible had actually worked. Perhaps he should have continued with his acting career.

He scooped up his ill-gotten gains and ran for the narrowing gap between earth and door, where he flung his burdens ahead of his own tumbling body, escaping much as he had entered.

Ping leapt to his feet and saw the retreating men turn into a wave of dust and heat. They were riding hard for some luckless destination to test their new invincible status.

Breath came hard as he dragged his spoils toward the large boulder to his right. To his great surprise and relief, the white stallion was still there.

Ping dropped to his knees and started to kiss the horse's feet, before thinking better of it. He looked into the animal's soulful eyes, then at its swishing tail. A smile crossed his lips as another facet of his plan popped into his head.

He bowed until his forehead touched the ground. "Oh noble one, please forgive me for what I am about to do, but I do it in the name of true love."

The stallion merely shook his lowered head.

☯

Ping bowed low, trying his best to look nonchalant.

The stone door had been ridiculously easy to open once he figured out the trick. Though he had never tried his hand at being a tailor, he had dated a royal dressmaker who had showed him many interesting ways to drape silk fabric. He hoped he looked suitably impressive.

He had found chemicals in the engineer's saddlebags and, with knowledge gained in his short but exciting career in fireworks manufacturing, he had managed his flash-powder entrance.

It felt good to unbraid his hair, and it seemed to fit the role.

"I am Chin Song Ping, a humble sorcerer from the celestial lands across the great water," he intoned.

Well, he had been a sorcerer's apprentice for a time, but he had hated the hours, and the potions gave him a rash.

"In my dreams, I saw a vision of the wonderful plan which you have wrought here in the Americas," he continued. "I thought how delightful and gratifying it would be to meet one with such a bold and devious mind." He laughed. "So, I determined I would drop by for a visit. I trust I haven't come at an inconvenient time."

Ping raised his head to see Moses, chest puffed out and a grin on his face, looking like a kid ready to show off new toys.

"Welcome, welcome!" Moses cried. "It isn't often I have a guest of your obvious intelligence and insight. Come, sit." He waved at the platform, and it became a table and two chairs. "I haven't much hospitality to offer. I suffer from a sensitivity to strong spirits and try to stay away ..."

From a fold of cloth, Ping pulled a bottle of fine sipping whiskey—another saddlebag find.

"… But perhaps I could make an exception for such a festive occasion." Moses' face lit up, and two glasses appeared on the table.

After a couple of toasts and some friendly chitchat, Ping sighed. "This is most pleasant, but I wonder if you have ever heard of this American game called poker? I've always wanted to learn it, and I do so enjoy a friendly game of chance."

No sooner had the words left the young man's lips than an unopened deck of cards appeared in Moses' hand. "I've heard of the game." A gleam of cold steel appeared in his eyes. "I'm told it's customary in poker to make wagers as you play. What shall we play for?"

From various folds of cloth, Ping withdrew diamonds, rubies and golden trinkets. Soon, a substantial pile had formed on the table. "I have these few baubles, will they do?" he asked innocently.

Moses' mouth watered. Ping was pleased the man hadn't recognized his own stolen treasure.

As Ping poured Moses a third drink, he noticed that the other man was starting to rock gently back and forth. For some reason, those who trafficked in magical doings often turned out to be cheap dates. Ping had once seen his magician master pass out while summoning a demon, under the influence, leaving him to entertain the monster for forty-five minutes, waiting for the spell to wear off.

After several losing hands, Ping's pile had diminished some and the bottle was half-empty. Moses raked in another pot and giggled sloppily.

"You know, Ping ol' buddy ol' pal, I like you! I'm going to let you in on a little secret. My name isn't really Moses Castle." Sly eyes darted around the room, making sure no one lurked nearby. Beside himself with glee, he continued. "It's actually Coyote! I'm something of a god around these parts."

Sweat broke out on Ping's upper lip, but his face remained calm. "A god?"

Coyote/Moses tilted back in his chair. "Yeah, well I was very big with a lot of the tribes who lived in these parts for thousands of years, but these days … white men, black men, even celestials such as yourself." He sighed. "It's all changed."

He looked wistfully at the bubbling pit. "But I've got my plan, and it's going pretty well so far. I'm thinking of renaming this whole part of the country Coyoteland. Has a nice ring, don't you think?"

Ping shuffled the cards and looked over his adversary's shoulder at Louise, who nodded in sad affirmation. "Hmm, a god, that must be very nice for you."

For a god, Ping thought, Coyote/Moses was a very poor cheat, but he continued to pretend not to notice. He lost a couple more hands before he said, as casually as he could, "I fear, oh great Coyote, that your plan is so wonderful in its subtlety that I don't fully grasp its logic." He laid aside two cards and got replacements. "Why didn't you just bestow your wondrous red sashes upon your native followers so they might rid this land of foreigners themselves?"

Coyote looked thoughtful, closing one eye and then the other in an effort to make the cards come into focus.

"I could have done that, but it would have been a rather mundane solution, don't you think? This way, my plan is intricate, subtle, like you said. I build my army of cowboys and send them out to pillage, kill and rape, lots of people dead or scared out of their gourds, high-tailing it back east. Eventually, the land will be free of foreign devils, a good thing all around I'd say."

The self-proclaimed god fanned himself with his cards. "Then, just when the cowboys think they have triumphed, I command all the sashes to choke their wearers like cloth pythons. They're all pieces cut from a single strip of cloth woven, fifty at a time, from the webs of Iktomi, the spider-spirit, a pal of mine. He had them lying around, so I sort of borrowed them last time I had dinner with him. Of course, last time I borrowed something without telling him, he set my tail on fire, but …" He blinked to clear the sweat that ran into his eyes. "What was I talking about?"

Ping took a sip of whiskey. "Something about slaughtering your minions?"

"Oh, yeah, yeah, yeah! I figure between the raping and gruesome deaths of the cowboys, no white man will ever dare set foot here again for at least a hundred years.

"After that, we get to the best part. I step forward, claim due credit, and the tribes regain their lands and worship me again, as I so richly deserve." His eyes misted over in nostalgia. "Now, I wouldn't be greedy, mind you. I'd just rule this southwest part of Arizona and maybe some of Mexico. Coyoteland! There's still plenty of territory for Iktomi and all the others who want to bring back the good old days. There are more out-of-work gods, spirits and unholy entities on this continent than most folks think. Of course they aren't as clever as me, but I say 'Be generous in victory.' Everyone wins!" He waggled his tongue between his lips. "Say, talking all this Chinese is getting to me. Would you mind if I make it so you can speak something easier—English, maybe Lakota?"

"English would be pleasant." A firecracker seemed to go off in his brain and then he was simply able to converse in English. "Thank you, I had meant to do just that before I came."

"A plan should be fun, don't you think! Here's to the plan." Coyote grabbed his glass and emptied it at a gulp.

Ping smiled a fragile grin of agreement and lost another poker hand.

Soon, both the whiskey and Ping's pile of treasure were nearly gone. He stretched and yawned as Coyote counted his winnings.

"I fear I haven't given you much of a challenge, and for that I apologize." Ping sighed and smiled warmly. "Perhaps it is because we play for mere baubles rather than things of true value and power."

Coyote's ears pricked up. "What do you have in mind?"

From a fold in his sleeve, Ping drew a long, stiff white hair that fairly glowed in the weird light. Summoning up all the knowledge he had gained during his time as a seller of rare antiquities, he began his pitch.

"This is a hair plucked from the chin of the great and holy Jade Emperor, may Buddha bless his name. Just before he ascended to heaven for his thousand-year reign, he called in his royal barber to groom him properly one last time. It is well-known that there are no decent barbers to be found in heaven. The barber, knowing the vanity of his lord, merely plucked one hair from the august personage's beard—this hair." Ping rolled the white hair between finger and thumb. "With that, he declared the emperor perfect and fit for heaven. From that day forth, whoever possesses this whisker is blessed with great handsomeness."

Coyote cocked an eyebrow at Ping and the hair.

"Ah, you think that I am good-looking but not devastatingly so." Ping continued, "But, before I acquired this hair, I was so ugly that women would throw rocks and children spat in my face. My warts had warts, and I looked as though someone had beaten me about the face with a chain. This face is the best the holy whisker could do for me. The mind reels at the glory it would bestow on one already as handsome as your own godly self."

With a drunken gleam in his eye, Coyote shoved his loot onto the table and said, "Let's play!"

Ping shook his head. "You insult me, sir! I offer a priceless wonder, and you would match it with mere baubles?"

"Name your stakes then!" Coyote cried, eyes locked on the hair.

Ping leisurely let his gaze wander around the room until it fell on Louise, sitting quietly in her cage. "The girl. She is pleasant to the eye, and I sense that she has some value to you." Ping nodded once, firmly.

Coyote plucked the key to her cage from around his neck and added it to the pile. Ping laid the white hair on top of the rest and shuffled the cards. Coyote cut the deck twice, one eye locked on his guest.

Ping dealt five cards to each of them and sat a moment, studying his hand. "The wager still seems somehow lacking. How would it suit you to wager something more personal, in addition to our existing bet?"

Coyote hunched into his cards and snarled, "Like what?"

"If you win, I will perform for you one service, no matter how unpleasant or demeaning. If I win, you pledge to do the same."

Coyote looked at his cards, then at the hair, then back at his hand. He smiled slightly. "Agreed."

"Ah, then I shall draw two cards. How many would you like?"

Moses Castle, the great Coyote, shook his head.

Ping drew two cards and frowned.

Slowly, dramatically, the Southwestern god lowered his cards to the table. He was holding two fives and three kings.

As he gazed into Coyote's eyes, Ping laid his cards down one at a time: a king, followed by an ace, and then another ace, and a third, and finally, with delicate precision, a fourth ace.

Coyote's face went white, even in the red light. "I've been tricked," he whispered. He shoved the table toward Ping and stood, taller and broader than he had been a moment before. He bellowed his rage. "I am Coyote! I'm the prince of tricksters, I don't *get* tricked!"

Ping jumped to his feet and hurried to the other side of the table, where he bowed in seeming supplication.

Nostrils flared, the trickster raised his hand to deliver a mighty blow to Ping's exposed back. Suddenly, the young man exploded forward and slammed into Coyote with a savage head butt to the god's groin.

The blow sent the god reeling backward until he stood pin-wheeling at the edge of the pool. For a moment, before plunging backward, screaming, into the natural cauldron, the look on his face seemed to say, "Not again." As he sunk, the pool burst forth in a great plume of hissing steam and water sloshed over the floor.

Ping snatched the key from the table and raced to Louise. The door was flung wide, and they embraced with a passion fueled by fear and relief. When they kissed, even the red lighting became more intense. The eventual need for air seemed the only thing that might part them.

"Ahem!" came a voice from over Ping's shoulder.

Ping shoved Louise behind him as he braced to continue the battle, though head butts were about the extent of his martial-arts repertoire.

"You didn't have to do that you know," Coyote said.

There on the table sat a sopping wet, slightly mangy, small coyote. Its fur was singed away in several places, and painful-looking blisters covered its reddened skin.

"I was just a little angry there and got carried away," Coyote said. "I wouldn't really have hurt you much. I always pay my debts. No need to get rough about it."

Ping bowed slightly but kept his narrowed eyes on Coyote. "My apologies."

"So, you have the girl. I guess I can always find another." A long-suffering look came over his canine features. "What service can I perform for you?"

Ping knit his brows in thought. There were so many things that a being like Coyote might do for him. "I humbly ask that you remove your spell of invincibility from the ruffians you call cowboys and never seek to use this evil plan again."

Coyote ran in tight, tiny circles on the tabletop, cursing in languages not yet invented. When he stopped, he looked as though he might cry.

"Oh, come on! Anything but that! I really like this plan, and you can't actually care all that much about what happens to these American white devils!"

Ping sighed. "Perhaps, perhaps not. But I intend to stay in this land for a while, and an army of homicidal, rapacious, invincible thugs might prove truly inconvenient at some point."

Coyote, sullen, licked at a blister on his left paw. "It was probably a dumb plan anyway."

The defeated-looking god turned to go with shoulders slumped, his tail tucked between his legs, but turned and gave a wide grin.

"I can turn off the sashes just by destroying the pool, so consider that taken care of." He vanished before Ping could lodge a complaint.

With a deep grumble, the cave started to shake itself apart. Echoing off the walls was a yipping noise that sounded suspiciously like laughter. Ping mentally kicked himself. He should have included a clause in their agreement about surviving all this.

☯

Ping shouted to Louise in his now-fluent English, "Run! Go swiftly to the cave's entrance. I left a trail of yellow thread to follow. This humble pilgrim shall join you there anon."

Louise, eyes wide in terror and bewilderment, rushed from the room. Ping spared just a moment to stare at the gold, jewels and single white hair on the table. No! He had to keep his mind on the bigger picture.

With practiced muscles, he leaped to the top of the cages and made a running dive into the vent hole on the wall. He smashed through the wicker grating like so much kindling and was gone. Yips of laughter spurred him on.

Louise made it to the entryway in good time, considering the fallen boulders she was forced to circumnavigate, but the stone wall was closed, of course. She had no idea how it worked, and Ping had neglected to share how the thing opened. It was a dead end. Her eyes stung from falling dust as she spent long minutes banging her fists on the stone edifice and feeling uselessly for some nonexistent locking mechanism.

She screamed as a huge section of the cave's ceiling crashed mere feet from where she stood. Finally, as dust filled her eyes and throat, a wracking cough shook her body and despair overtook her. She sat down hard and cried, with rocks and dirt falling around her.

With all that had happened to her in the past few months, being snatched from her home, the hideous deaths, the abuse ... Why had she foolishly pinned her hopes on the smile of a handsome stranger? A glimmer of hope, snatched away like a shiny penny that turns out to be a brass slug—it was too much.

Then out of the dust and debris came a sound, "Awooooo!"

The stone door began to shiver and move.

"Awoooooooooo!" louder this time.

Ping broke through the falling debris, wearing only tattered pants and a layer of dust. He blinked to clear his vision and coughed dryly between howls. Behind him, he dragged an enormous silk bundle that would have given Father Christmas a hernia.

Their kiss was no less passionate this time, though necessarily shorter. He motioned that she should help drag the bundle. She grunted at the weight but was overjoyed by the shaft of sunlight that filtered under the great stone and the first whiff of fresh air that streamed in under the slowly rising door.

"Stay close. I fear that calamity may come just as easily in the last hand as in the first." Ping choked through the grit that still filled the air.

She grinned fiercely and replied, "You're like a hero from

some ol' story book, you know that?"

The door lifted only about a foot and a half from the ground, and there it stopped.

"Crawl!" he croaked and pushed Louise through the opening.

With tears in his eyes, he poured out the contents of his bundle until it looked like it might squeeze through. He would have to content himself with being very rich instead of filthy rich.

He emerged into the sunlight where Louise waited. She pulled on the shrunken sack of treasure, understanding the need to keep moving for fear that the mountain itself would shake apart onto their heads. Coyote was petty and spiteful, but he was also thorough.

They reached the brush-covered boulder that hid the white stallion as the door fell ponderously under its own weight. It seemed to take half the cliff side with it.

Louise laughed and wrapped her arms around Ping, smothering him in kisses and tears of joy. Ping looked relieved and dazed. He stared, goggle-eyed at the fallen wall of stone. The yips of Coyote's laughter no longer echoed in his ears.

"We made it." His eyes rolled up into his head as he fainted dead away into Louise's strong arms.

Out somewhere in the merciless Arizona desert, a scraggly gray form chewed on a hapless rodent he had caught for dinner. As he masticated, he puzzled over a long white hair clutched between his paws. He couldn't make more of his invincible cowboys, but a new plan already was forming in his tiny brain. He had once heard an old medicine woman's prophecy about a place, in the land called Holy-Wood, where one day the beautiful and handsome would rule as kings and queens. When that day came, he would be the handsomest of all and therefore a king among kings. That sounded pretty good. He studied the hair more closely and wondered how to get the darned thing to work.

All five members of Tommy's audience had broken into raucous laughter so loud that a guard from the other room came in brandishing a rifle. This, of course, caused even more laughter. The guard slammed the door behind him muttering a string of curses in German.

"Ya know," Russ said, "that magical language translating trick sure would help with understanding those guys." He rubbed his bandaged eyes till Tommy gently pulled his hands away.

"If you want any chance at all of those eyes healing, you better not rub them."

"Yeah?" Russ' mood instantly darkened. "Is there any chance that they'll heal up tonight? I don't see tomorrow being much of an option. Blind and hungry—gosh what a swell way to spend what could be my last night on Earth."

Tommy smiled gently. Fred spoke up with a little laugh. "You say you're hungry? Shoot, I bet you never been really hungry. I thought I knew all about hunger before Tommy told me that ghost story about ol' Ping.

Private Duke, the youngest one there, spoke out. "Damn, I love ghost stories! C'mon Tommy, tell us something scary."

Tommy sat back down and rubbed his hands together. "I don't know how scary this is but I looked up Donner in the encyclopedia and at least that part's true. They even had a paragraph about hungry ghosts but only as a Chinese myth."

Sergeant Cole shifted his splinted leg into a better position. "Okay, now you have got me hooked, I have some cousins named Donner."

"By now it will come as no surprise that this one is called…"

## CHIN SONG PING AND THE HUNGRY GHOSTS
### SIERRA NEVADA MOUNTAINS: 1884

Ping hated mules more than he hated horses. "Esmerelda, I offer fair warning, if you do not move this instant, I shall be

126

forced to live up to my job title as mule-skinner ... literally. I shall have no qualms about turning your hide into several pairs of unfashionable boots."

Esmerelda swung her head from side to side emitting a loud, long bray that sounded like laughter to Ping's untrained ear. There were four mules in the team that pulled the dynamite wagon Ping was driving through the Sierra Mountains, but Esmerelda was the lead. When she decided it was time for a break, the rest of the mule union went along with her.

This was Ping's first actual encounter with mules, despite the lies he had told to get this job. In the five years Ping had roamed the United States, after leaving his native China, he had never met a horse that liked him. He had been kicked, bitten, thrown and just plain ignored ... but at least horses were noble creatures. He understood their disdain of a scoundrel such as himself. Mules, however, were scruffy and foul smelling ... Ping considered them in no way his social betters. And, he hated the way they laughed at him.

"God damn it, Ping." Harry, the other driver, and Ping's boss on this expedition, raised up from his nap among the crates of explosives. "You are the worst mule-skinner I've ever seen."

Ping jiggled the reins furiously. "It is not my fault that you have recruited the most obstinate team of mules in Nevada. I am accustomed to working with a more professional class of jackass." In truth, Ping knew he would never have been hired if *anyone* else had volunteered.

Harry shifted, careful to protect his right arm encased in a colorful bandana sling. "Crap! Maybe it's just as well. Sun's getting low and it don't hardly make no sense to go falling off this mountain, with all this dynamite, in the dark." He chuckled softly. "Hell, I'd hate to have to explain something like that to ol' Saint Peter… damned embarrassing."

Ping knew this referred to one of the Christian deities. As much as the people in this land professed to believe in only one god, they certainly invoked any number of them when worked up. Jesus, Mary, plain old God, and occasionally this Peter, were all fervently advocated by practitioners of this religion. It made little sense to Ping, but then few religions did.

Camp was a simple affair, bedrolls and a cooking fire over which Ping made pan biscuits. It bothered him that after two months as a cook in an Oregon timber camp, biscuits were still the only thing he could reliably make that was edible. He had lost a tiny chunk of ear to the thrown axe that had served as a termination notice to that career. He offered Harry a plate of excellent biscuits and barely palatable beans.

"Harry, I apologize for my earlier impudence. I know that I am a disappointment to you with regards to my driving skills ... My dear mother felt the same about me in general."

Harry spit a bit of gravel out of his mouthful of beans. "Well, mules will have that effect on a man. Fact is I'm just glad I finally found someone to share the chore with. Ain't no way I could have got 'er done alone with this busted wing." He moved his sling so he could hold the plate more easily. "This time of year, over this here pass ... Hell, I wouldn't do it if they hadn't waggled that huge bonus in front of me."

Ping had his own reasons for taking the job but... "Why, exactly is that, oh honorable boss?"

"Why, the Donner party, you ignorant heathen." Ping had learned to ignore casual cultural insults. He would have little time for anything else had he not. "Thank you for this worthy information, now what sort of party is a Donner party?"

Harry set down his plate and rubbed his hands together, a wicked gleam in his eyes. "Now, that is a tale not for the faint of heart."

Ping leaned back and gnawed on his biscuit.

"Way I heard it, back in '46 a feller named George Donner set out to lead a whole passel of folks from Missouri to the Promised Land in California. George got hold of some bad advice and had them folks wandering around Utah like the children of Israel ... that's in the bible. It added a couple of months to their travels. By this time they'd lost a bunch of cattle and horses and were just desperate to get across the Sierra-Nevada Mountains any way they could before winter set in. True to form, old Donner had them head up into the mountains and straight into the worst winter in history. Well, sir, they got stuck ... right about where we are sitting at this very moment ... and there they stayed."

Ping's eyes narrowed. He didn't care for the direction this story was headed.

"There were a bunch of rescue attempts but the snow up here was as high as Abe Lincoln in that top-hat of his. Months went by, and the food those folks had brought was long gone. They ate up the livestock and chewed on boot-leather and belts. In the end, only about half those folks made it out alive. Why don't you ask me how those poor souls managed to survive that awful winter?"

"I feel certain you will illuminate me whether I ask it of you or not." Ping set down his plate and shoved it gingerly to one side.

"They survived by eating the ones who didn't make it! Ain't that something?"

Ping pinched the bridge of his nose. "Why take this route then? Are there not others we might have taken? Is this not late October with the whiff of snow already in the air? Are you quite insane?"

Harry laughed and swallowed a mouthful of biscuit. "Well now, let's see. There was cheap dynamite in Nevada and hardly no dynamite in California, where the Central Pacific is blasting away, trying to poke a hole for the railroad to go through these here mountains. And, this was the quickest way to get 'twixt the two. At least three others lit out, loaded with explosives, just like us, but they took the southern route. We can beat them by a week and make out like bandits selling this stuff."

Without a word, Ping rounded up his few possessions, which he tied in a bundle and slung it over his back. Running in the dark was risky but his eyesight was keen and he was very nimble. Most of the way was downhill and if he maintained a steady trot he felt sure he could reach safety within three days. Despite everything Ping had seen in his short life, he was not a superstitious man. Ghost tales meant nothing to him. And, while tales of cannibalism were repulsive, they didn't stir any real terror in his breast. What he could not abide was missing his business in San Francisco. Also, he did not relish the thought of spending the winter in such a god-forsaken place subsisting on fillet of Harry Dodge and Esmerelda stew.

"Hey, wait! Where in the Sam Hill do you think you're going? We got us a contract." Harry was on his feet and all humor had fled his eyes. "Look, winter is still a couple of weeks off. I can feel it in my bones and my bones ain't hardly never wrong. We'll be sitting pretty in California long before then."

Ping bowed low. "I fear I do not know your bones well enough to trust them. I know Esmerelda just well enough to not trust my life on her speed. What I do trust is my own cowardice. It has seldom failed me." He turned to walk off.

"I'll double… triple your wages."

Ping halted. "My cowardice could be bought off with nothing short of a percentage of the coming reward." It would certainly be better to arrive in San Francisco as a man of means rather than as a ragged pilgrim, weary from his trek and empty of pocket.

It was a great moral dilemma for both Ping and Harry Dodge, survival versus the cleansing power of greed.

"I'll go twenty-five, seventy-five and not a penny more, you thieving owl-hoot." Dodge stuck out his hand to the young Chinese man.

Ping eyed the hand like it stank of leprosy. "A thirty, seventy split would do much more to bolster my waning courage." Ping could almost hear the beads of the abacus in the man's head as he calculated the plusses and minuses of the situation.

Finally Harry's eyes came to a sharp focus and a grudging grin split his face. "Done! Put her there, partner."

Ping was sure that his luck was finally turning. In one week's time San Francisco was to host the largest F'an T'an tournament ever to be held in America and Ping just had to be there. Now he might even do so in style.

In recent years he had come to prefer poker to the venerable Chinese game but still… There were rumors that the Imperial Nephew himself might attend, incognito of course, and his pockets were deep indeed. All of Ping's once-fabulous fortune had been long since pissed away. He saw this as a chance to reclaim his standing as a man of substance, and surely if he were once again wealthy he could win back his lovely Louise.

For two years Ping and Louise had lived high on the riches

he had won in a poker game with the trickster-god, Coyote. When the last of it was gone they had been happy living by their wits, turning a mostly-legal dollar here and there. Louise, granddaughter of a Voodoo Queen, seemed as well suited to this life of adventure as he was himself.

Then, two weeks ago, Ping had bet everything he had on a horse race. Unfortunately his luck with the equine species had run true to form and he lost everything. Even more unfortunately, that "everything" included Louise. She was not pleased to be used as barter in this age where slavery was supposedly long dead. When the winner showed up to collect his due, she bought herself back with the money she had squirreled away hidden from Ping's impulses. Then she purchased the man's pistol from him and went to find Ping.

Even here, lying under the stars, with Harry snoring loudly nearby, Ping was sure that, in her heart, Louise still loved him ... why else would she have missed him six times?

☯

It was still the dead of night when Ping's slumber was rudely interrupted by Esmerelda. Even Ping could tell she was not laughing this time.

By the dying embers of the fire, Ping could see his new partner sitting upright in his bedroll, His one good hand in the air and eyes wide with terror. Arrayed around the camp were unshaven men in large hats, with large guns. Ping knew the hats were called sombreros which probably meant that the men were Mexican bandits. He was pretty sure about the bandit part because one of the men had a pistol pointed at Harry's head and another had a shotgun pointed at Ping.

There were several bandits, most of them rummaging through the wagon.

"Paco, there ain't no gold here. The gringos got a wagon full of dynamite." A bandit jumped down from the wagon, slapping his hands together in disgust. "I say we shoot them and get back to that cabin. It's damned cold out here!"

The one with the shotgun pushed back his sombrero and scratched furiously at his scalp. "Madre! What sort of fool carts explosives through the mountains this time of year?"

Harry looked unable to answer so Ping stood slowly and

bowed low to the one with the shotgun. He seemed to be in charge. "If we have trespassed unknowingly on your lands, we humbly beg forgiveness. The most fearful load of dynamite, which you have correctly divined is not gold, is bound for California and the railroad."

The men all had a good laugh at Ping's explanation. Paco moved the weapon away from Ping. "Our land? Do we look like fur trappers? I am Paco Gonzales and these are my men, surely you have heard us?"

Ping looked thoughtful for a moment then shrugged his shoulders. "I fear I have not."

The bandit leader looked inquiringly at Harry, who shook his head reluctantly.

"Look, that one is ignorant and has a broken arm. What good is he? Kill him."

Before Ping could protest, a shot rang out and Harry Dodge slumped sideways. Blood poured from the large hole in his head, his eyes still wide open, now and for eternity.

Gonzales turned back to Ping. "Have you heard of me now, shit-for-brains?"

The young Chinese man forced back the bile that was rising in his throat. "You are Paco Gonzales, emperor of bandits, and I assume I will soon be dead."

The bandit came over and patted Ping's cheek. "I like you. You're a funny fellow." Gonzales then began yelling orders at his men. "Hide the mules and bring the food but leave the wagon here. Tomorrow we will unload it and try to finally get the hell out of here." A wind moaned slowly through the pine trees and all the bandits froze in fear. "¡Vamonos! I don't want to be standing out here scratching my cajones when the ghosts get here. We have to get back to the cabin pronto."

Ping followed along submissively, but not before pulling Harry's blanket over the dead man's face. Oddly, Esmerelda would only let herself be led by Ping.

☯

The cabin was run down but solid. More than that, it was relatively warm. Ping was at least glad not to be sleeping outside again. The bandits dug into the stolen food supplies like they hadn't eaten in days.

Ping decided that his lot could hardly worsen by trying to satisfy his curiosity about what was going on. He bowed to the bandit chief. "Forgive my ignorance, but why is the emperor of bandits holed up in this shabby excuse for a palace, so far from his border kingdom? And, though I see saddles strewn around, why are there no horses tied outside."

Paco wiped bean juice from his mustache. "You ask a lot of questions, but I still like you so I will answer them." He kicked at a small man shoveling rice into his face. "We are here because of Ramon … who I should kill, but he is my sister's worthless husband … had a brilliant idea to escape the Federales chasing us. Hide in the mountains, he said. We can lose them, he said. We did lose them eventually, but it took three days and got us hopelessly lost. The horses were eaten by ghosts."

Ghosts? Yes, the man had mentioned ghosts before. Ping had thought it merely part of the man's colorful use of language. "I see. In China we had feasts for hungry ghosts. My mother would leave out plates of food to appease them, but I've never heard of any ghosts that actually ate the offerings. It was more about helping those who were unsatisfied and unfulfilled in life who took these feelings with them into the next life."

Gonzales stared at Ping, open mouthed. "I don't think these ghosts are going to be bought off by a couple of plates of rice and beans. When we found this cabin a week ago, I thought we'd stay the night and leave the next morning. That night we tied up the horses and were awakened by their screams in the middle of the night. They were being torn apart by things we could barely make out in the dark. Two of my men ran out to save the horses." His voice got quiet and the symphony of slurps and gulps died down as he continued the story. "They were torn apart for their trouble, a snack for the hungry ghosts. We locked ourselves in and said our rosaries. Then they came through the walls like they weren't even there, and whispered to us. I don't know what they were saying, but at least they didn't eat us. They won't eat us in here." The men looked at the walls and trembled. "Next morning we found only the bones of the men and horses. We ran down the mountain. It was daylight. What sort of self-respecting ghost comes out in the

daytime? But, there they were. They caught Felipe and ate him
while the rest of us ran back for this cabin. Here we sat for a
week until we saw your campfire an hour ago."

Ping had seen many strange things and these did not seem
like fanciful men prone to making up stories. "Perhaps the
ghosts have left. You were able to go to and from our camp
without being molested."

The bandit closed his eyes and cringed. "I don't think
they've left, señor."

Ping felt his heart go cold then a phantom hand came out
of the front of his chest. The rest of the arm followed suit as
a translucent form crawled through him. Ping screamed. The
cabin was filled with wraith-like forms, coming through the
walls and ceiling. The dimly lit room was alive with loud, insistent and incoherent whispering, audible even over the screams
of the tortured bandits. Ping folded himself up like a babe in its
womb but nothing could shut out the dry rasps of tongues long
dead. He felt the cold go through him several times and when
he dared open an eye there was a gaunt face staring back. It
had once been a woman's face. Her cheeks were sunken and
her eyes were hidden by the caves of her eye sockets. Ping saw
the room beyond her clearly as through smoked glass. Her lips
trembled with a passionate need to be heard.

"I fear I cannot understand you O fearsome spirit," Ping
stuttered. "Please speak more clearly and I will do whatever
you ask."

The ghost screeched in dry frustration but Ping had an
idea. "I believe there is one who might help us understand
each other. Look on the trail above here for the spirit of Harry
Dodge. He has died only recently and may yet speak the language of the living."

Suddenly the room contained only the living once again.
All around, Ping heard terrified moans and his nose caught
the acrid stench of urine. He now understood too well both
reactions. Ramon sat rocking back and forth, knees drawn into
his chest. Only Paco Gonzales seemed to still possess all his
faculties.

"That was a short one." The bandit stuck out his chin
defiantly.

After several minutes, the clean-up began. What supplies they had had been knocked over in the men's thrashings to escape the whispers from Hell. It seemed futile but at least Gonzales was a good enough leader to realize that the routine of work could help counteract the horrors of the last quarter hour.

Ping straightened up the saddles piled in one corner and quietly went through saddlebags to see if they might contain anything useful... though what that would be he had no idea. Then, without warning, Harry Dodge appeared, sitting comfortably on the topmost saddle. He looked well, both arms in good working order.

"Just because I made you my partner don't give you the privilege to whistle me up any time you want. I was half way to the Pearly Gates when that skinny lady found me."

Ping fell over backwards and several bandits rushed over to see what had happened.

Paco looked around nervously. "What's the matter, Chino, afraid of a few little ghosts?" This got the expected laughter from his men.

Ping stuttered, "Can't you see him? Harry! You shot him a while ago."

Harry shifted on the saddle. "Look, Ping, I don't give a rat's ass about these Mexican hooligans, but I figure I owe you for getting you into this mess. Tell them to shut up so we can talk."

Ping turned to Gonzales. "The spirit of Harry has asked that you shut up... please. He has spoken to the other ghosts and may be able to help."

The bandit chief didn't look happy about it but he quieted his men. "Tell your friend that I'm sorry I had him shot." Ping just shushed him.

"That's better. As I said, I was halfway to Heaven when I got stopped by a woman leading the mangiest bunch of ghosts I ever laid eyes on. You remember I told you about the Donner party?"

Ping nodded. "Are these then the poor unfortunates who were eaten by their friends?"

"Hell no. These are the folks that did the eating. This is

the cabin where they stayed that winter and when the survivors died of natural causes, years later, their souls were drawn back here. Seems they're bound to this shack where they are damned to eternal hunger. If you're just passing through they have to let you be, but if you use their cabin you're fair game."

"I was dragged here against my will, surely they would not eat me?" Ping felt indignant. This wasn't fair on any level.

"Partner, they didn't make the rules, they just follow them. This here damned cabin saved their lives and now it damns them for eternity." Harry scratched his ghostly head. "If I see God I'll ask him about this, but till then it looks like your best bet is to blow your brains out while you're safe inside here. At least that way you won't become no hungry ghost yourself. Well, I got me some harp lessons to get to." And the ghost of Harry Dodge disappeared as quickly as it had come.

Ping stood quietly for a moment, his head hanging low he turned to Gonzales and his band. "Harry says we should all kill ourselves so at least our souls might remain free." There was a low growl of grumbling at this. Ping raised his head and gave a wolf-like smile to the bandits. "I do not care for this plan at all, and have thought of another. If the emperor of bandits will trust a humble scoundrel such as myself, we might just get out of this with our skins."

☯

Ping patted his makeshift bundle carefully. He adjusted it again to make sure he would have easy access to it without crushing the contents. "Have the spirits come back yet?"

Ramon stood at the dirty, smudged window keeping lookout. "Si. They are gathering now, it won't be long."

Ping turned to the young bandit, Luis, who had been chosen as the best runner and helped the man adjust his bundle. "Remember, head downhill wherever possible." Luis bobbed his head vigorously in affirmation, though his eyes were wide in terror. "Do not use your ammunition to excess, it must last you." Ping had his doubts about the man.

"We all know our parts. Don't be such a mother hen." Paco was getting anxious for things to get started "I still don't see why we can't use the mules? Francisco can hitch up a team faster than anyone you've ever seen."

Ping exhaled nervously ... his plan seemed less brilliant with each passing second. "I do not doubt the worthy Francisco's skill or speed, only the work ethics the stubborn Esmerelda."

Ramon tugged the ragged curtains back over the window. "Madre! Here they come." He instinctively reached for the worn rosary beads he knew very well were no longer there.

Gonzales slapped Ping on the shoulder and grabbed for the door handle. "I'll see you in Hell, amigo."

As the door was flung open Ping plunged through. "I hope not." He said as he grabbed at the overhang on the porch. He let his momentum swing him in an easy arc up onto the roof. Though the shingles clattered under his feet, the roof held under his weight. He took this as a very good omen. He climbed swiftly up to the peak where he could steady himself. He was pleased to see that his skills as an acrobat had not eroded too badly. He often thought he would be a great acrobat playing in the pleasure halls of Beijing if he had not been caught in bed with the head acrobat's wife. *Sigh.*

As hoped, more than half the ghosts veered off to attack Ping. He was no longer protected from their appetites by the wooden walls. They had almost reached him when he plucked something warm and round out of his bundle. He threw it hard as he could and the ghosts followed it. What hungry being, dead or alive would not prefer a warm biscuit to a stringy acrobat.

There had been some debate as to whether biscuits or tortillas would be the best distraction, but it was Ramon who reminded everyone that Missouri ghosts might not know what a tortilla was. Though the dough preparation and baking conditions were below Ping's usual standards, the bread had come out quite light and fluffy.

Ping glanced down the slope of the roof in time to see Luis sprint from the cabin, throwing biscuits as he went. He wanted to shout *save your ammunition*, but he had more pressing matters of his own to attend to. The ghosts were heading back his way.

He rolled down the backside of the roof and sprang into the gnarled pines that surrounded the area. The ghosts were almost on him when he launched another flour and lard missile. Like a squirrel, he jumped nimbly to another tree and then another, where he was surprised by a lone ghost and dropped a biscuit. Fortunately the ghost followed the falling food. Ping knew that this was a combined game of fetch and tag, and that he'd have to be more careful if he wanted to win it. Before his next leap, he saw Gonzales and the rest of the bandits jogging up the slope on their assigned mission. Good.

Ping kept to the trees, flinging biscuits only as needed. That the apparitions gave off a faint glow was just enough to keep track of them, and stay one step ahead. It had been a long while since he had had this much exercise and it was beginning to show. He had barely made his last jump. He could tell the land was sloping downward and saw that the trees came to an abrupt end ahead. Buddha be praised.

From somewhere left of him he heard a scream and the sounds of struggle. Ping threw another biscuit and headed for the scream.

From his perch he saw Luis lying still on the ground, one leg torn off his body and half his face missing. Three of the ghosts gnawed at the bandit's flesh but the rest were fighting over the biscuits that had fallen out of his bag. Ping dropped lightly to the ground.

It was a horrifying tableau but Ping felt only pity for the ghosts. They were not evil demons, but ordinary people who had lost their way, and were now eternally cursed for that mistake. He had felt like a hungry ghost himself since his mother had thrown him out at fourteen, telling him that he would never amount to anything. His aspirations to be a great gambler, or acrobat, or cook, or any of the dozens of other failed careers he had aspired to over the years, were just his way of showing the world that he was not worthless. How could anyone, how could Louise, love a man who was worthless?

As the spirits finished their feast, he saw the rest of the ghosts were returning from above. Tears welled up in Ping's eyes as he held up a biscuit and yelled. "I am hungry too! Catch me or I shall eat these wonderful biscuits all by myself and fart at you for your efforts." He bit into the biscuit and took off running in the direction he had seen the forest end. Not his most rousing speech but it served the purpose, the ghosts were all hot on his heels.

Ping didn't throw any more tasty grenades but relied instead on speed. Before long he felt icy scratches on his back and tucked himself into a roll sideways. He bounded spryly to his feet and pulled out a length of cord comprised of wooden beads and worn crucifixes. The cord clattered as he twirled it above his head. The ghosts gave the beaded string a wide berth, unsure of what Ping was up to now.

He had their attention, now for the pitch. "You do well to fear these holy relics, Rosaries personally blessed by the head Pope man in Rome. They would burn the flesh off such wretches as you have become... if you had flesh. Saint Frances the sissy asked for a holy communion dance with your Jesus himself while wearing these. Peter, Paul, and Mary sang at their wedding." He was quickly exhausting his meager knowledge of Christianity, but the shades seemed to maintain their respectful distance as he twirled his "holy relic" in a ragged figure eight. Suddenly, one of the ghosts surged forward into the path of the twirling beads. Whether the move was brave or suicidal on the ghost's part, Ping could not say, but the effect was not unexpected. Nothing happened.

Of all the curse words Ping knew, an American one seemed most appropriate at that particular minute. "Shit!" Ping hurled the cord at the ghosts and ran. It couldn't be far, and then, there it was right ahead of him. He skidded to a stop, amid flying gravel, just short of the precipice of the cliff looming before him. He plucked off the bundle and spun in place to build momentum before he threw the thing far out into the valley below. Once again the ghosts, slaves to their baser instincts, ignored him and went chasing after the bag of biscuits.

Ping put his hands on his knees and gulped lungs-full of the cold night air. It would be a while before the ghosts found the bag, but they would find it. They might spend some time squabbling over its contents, but they would be back eventually. Ping stripped off his wool coat and threw it into the valley after the specters. With one last deep breath he turned. He would be more than warm enough running back up the mountain.

☯

Paco Gonzales cracked his whip to no avail. The mules had decided to stop a couple of hundred feet from the cabin and could be coaxed no further. "You motherless offspring of a jack-rabbit and a dead horse, move! I am the driver, I have the whip. I say you move or I swear I will shoot you dead and maybe then you'll move."

This was the scene Ping witnessed as he rounded the cabin. He stopped, breathing deeply through his nose. Had his instructions not been clear? Apparently not to an egotistical, maniacal bandit leader, eager to show everyone that he would not be bossed around. Ping stalked straight to Gonzales and raised a furious finger into his face. The bandit at least had the good grace to turn an embarrassed crimson. Ping counted backwards from ten to one in Chinese before he turned and stalked over to Esmerelda. He started to point his finger at the mule but realized the futility, so he stretched up onto his toes to whisper in the mule's ear.

The wagon lurched forward as Esmerelda and her teammates strained at their harnesses. Ping jumped on her back as the wagon gained speed. They had almost reached the structure when Ping urged the mules sharply to the right. As a result, the wagon slid sideways into the building at full speed, destroying half the wall as it did so, but, miraculously, not exploding.

All the bandits let out a loud whoop and started grabbing crates of dynamite to plant strategically around the cabin, inside and out. This had to be done right if there was to be any chance of success.

Gonzales was measuring out lengths of fuse but seemed torn about their lengths. "I don't have much experience with this sort of thing, amigo. Should I make them long or short?"

Ping had unhitched the mules and slapped their flanks to send them on their way. In the distance there was an angry wail which got louder by the second. "I think short fuses would be most excellent."

Once the dynamite had been placed, all the bandits gathered around Ping as their chief lit the fuse. Ping could see they had come to look to him for guidance. What would a great leader say at such a time? *Run?* Yes that seemed sound advice. "RUN!"

It became a madhouse. The vengeful ghosts came screaming in as the bandits dispersed in all directions, often running into each other. Ping made for a large boulder set some distance to the left of the house. He heard screams behind him but did not turn to discover the screamers' identities. He focused all his energy into his aching leg muscles. Something cold ripped through his shin and he stumbled. He rolled over to see the spirit that had slashed him wheel around to claim his prize. Ping pulled a half-eaten biscuit out of his pants pocket and threw it back toward the cabin. Once again, hunger trumped revenge and Ping crawled to the boulder. With much effort he made it to the stony top and let himself drop to the other side.

He lay there huffing, looking up at the sky when he saw a glowing shape glide over the boulder and descend toward him. He had no more running in him. The thing drifted closer and Ping wanted to scream. Finally the apparition was almost nose to nose when he realized it was the ghost woman he had tried to communicate with earlier in the cabin. Her mouth opened and a strained whisper, dryer than a grave, came forth. "Thank you." She kissed his forehead.

And then the world exploded.

A wagonload of dynamite was an awful lot of dynamite. The huge boulder Ping had hoped would protect him rocked back and forth threatening to crush him at any moment. Then he could see nothing for the smoke and falling debris. After several minutes he started the task of digging himself out of the gravel heap that had come to rest on him. He stood tenuously, slowly putting weight on his injured leg. No major damage, thank Buddha. He staggered his way around the boulder to see what was left of the cursed cabin.

There was only a large hole, a crater, to give any credence to its once having existed. Then, in the smoke, he saw Gonzales and two of his men. Their clothes were in tatters and covered in dirt but they all limped toward Ping.

"Pretty good thinking for a shit-for-brains chino," the chief laughed through his coughing, "If you can't kill a ghost, kill the place that keeps them hanging around." He bent over to pick up a shredded sombrero lying at his feet and put it on Ping's head. "What do you think? You would make one great bandit.

What a team you and I would make."

Ping removed the hat and bowed as he handed it back to Paco. "It is a most kind offer, coming from the emperor of bandits as it does, but I have business back in Nevada. It is time I stopped being a hungry ghost."

Paco dusted himself off with the sombrero. "Well, if you change your mind, my throne room is just the other side of the Rio Grande." He motioned to his men. "Play-time is all over, muchachos, we got us some mules to catch."

Ping sat down on the rim of the crater and watched the bandits disappear into the smoke. After a time he felt a nuzzling on his neck and turned to see Esmerelda and a faint figure standing beside her.

The figure spoke in a dry whisper. "What in tar-nation did you say to this critter to get her moving?"

"Harry!" Ping sprang to his feet. "Why are you not in your Christian Heaven?"

One corner of the ghost's mouth quirked up. "I might have stretched the truth a mite about being at the Pearly Gates and all. I just been sort of fading away here and I don't know what's next no more than the man in the moon. So, what did you say?"

Ping stroked the mule's coarse gray fur. "I told her that there was a very large sugar cube inside the house and that an Arabian stallion was about to eat all of it if she did not hurry."

Harry's laugh sounded like rolling sagebrush. "I recon that'd get 'er done." Then he was gone.

The ride back to Nevada was a cold one without a winter coat, but Ping kept himself close to Esmerelda's neck to share her warmth. They had come to an understanding, of sorts, back at the crater and there had been no work stoppages since.

Ping stood in the early morning hours, staring up at the window of the Carson City hotel where he and Louise had lived, before his hasty exodus.

Surely she had already moved on, or perhaps she lay up there sleeping in the arms of another … a man who would certainly shoot him on sight.

Perhaps he should steal some clothing and a good breakfast before knocking on door number 218?

No.

He knew that despite the wisdom gleaned from the hungry ghosts, he would always be a gambler. He licked his palms and slicked back his hair. This was a hand he must play. He was done with bluffing.

There wasn't a lot of laughter after Tommy finished. Even Tommy was thinking about what death meant.

"You know," Private Winston drawled. "In all these here stories you mention Louise, who I take is your grandmother, but don't you have any stories about her? I get that Ping was, or is, quite a character but what did he see so special about her?"

Tommy breathed in a long, deep, cold breath but his memories served to warm that air till a smile dominated his face once again. "Louise and Ping are both still alive, last time I saw them at least. She's my Granny and I guess all Grannies are pretty wonderful when you're a little kid." He reached in under his shirt and withdrew a small pouch on a string. "When I left, she gave me this and told me that if I was ever in a pickle I should wave this around my head three times and call her name. She never talked much about herself but she could go on for hours about hoodoo and voodoo. Not like things to scare us but to let us know there was a whole big world hidden behind the stuff we saw every day. She used to say that you can't look out a window unless you can fling open the curtains."

"Sounds like my Grandma," Corporal Tragger intoned.

Winston jumped to his feet. "Well, get at it!"

"What?" Tommy asked.

"If this don't qualify as a sure enough pickle then I don't know what does." Winston gestured for everyone to stand up. Duke helped Tragger to his feet and the sergeant let Fred give him a hand. Only Tommy remained seated.

"Yeah, a joke's a joke, and I get it. They're stories. You can laugh at Ping, he loves the attention, but I won't have you guys making fun of Granny Louise."

Sergeant Cole put his hand on Tommy's shoulder. "Do you know what desperate Times call for? Desperate measures, that's what." Five heads nodded in agreement. "I have seen guys clutch a rabbit's foot with bombs falling all around him and not get a scratch. Was it the rabbit's foot saved him? Maybe not, but having something to cling to didn't hurt things either."

Tommy stood. "Here goes then." He swung the pouch slowly over his head as the men chanted, "One, Two, Three." Then all together they shouted "LOUISE!"

A guard ducked his head in to see what the commotion was, but quickly rolled his eyes and retreated. The men held hands in a circle. Whatever made them different to each other out in the world had disappeared by flickering candlelight. This night they were family.

Tommy nodded his head solemnly. "There is one of Grandfather Ping's tall tales that addresses who she was when she was younger. Granny hated it and wouldn't let him tell it when she was around. But there is some nudity in it so I don't know if Private Duke is old enough to hear it."

Duke threw his gloves at Tommy and everyone cracked up.

"So then, if I recall correctly this one is called..."

## CHIN SONG PING AND THE MOJO UPRISING
### NEW ORLEANS: 1886

Torches were everywhere, lighting the grotesque, nightmare figures that danced and pranced all around Ping and Louise. Flotillas of garishly festooned behemoths rolled serenely by as brassy music and strident voices pounded through their heads.

Yet, in all this pandemonium Ping's attention was drawn only to the tall young woman right in front of him, or rather her plump, ripe breasts which she had laughingly and suddenly bared for all to see. Ping cocked his head back and forth for a more three dimensional view of the phenomenon as showers of sparkling beads and trinkets were pelted upon her from all sides.

"This is the most peculiar religious celebration in which I have ever participated," Ping shouted. "Even the dragon parades of my youth pale in comparison."

Louise laughed and twirled around. "Shoot, I'd be hikin' my blouse too if it weren't for this here baby belly of mine." She took Ping's hand and placed it on her stomach. "See, he's already dancin' and he ain't even been born yet." She snagged a strand of beads out of the air and slipped them around Ping's neck.

"This here's Mardi Gras, Fat Tuesday" she squealed. "Folks do all this so they got something decent to regret. That way they can repent from it when Lent comes around."

Ping nodded sagely. "Atonement is a worthy goal on the winding road of enlightenment. I do see the logic in making one's ultimate redemption all the more gratifying with such innocent sins to provide savor to the soul. I have certainly had my own share of indiscretions along my path.

Louise laughed and yelled. "I can't hear a word you are sayin'."

Off to his left another woman lifted her top to show her zeal to enhance her forthcoming repentance. So Ping, ever eager to fit into his new American home, dropped his silken pants around his ankles and stood on his head. The bare breasted woman screamed. "My sweet baby Jesus! Someone save me from this heathen devil."

A large man staggered forward, his gold bird mask hitched up onto his forehead, he swung a beefy fist at Ping, now on his feet once again. The young man ducked the blow easily but forgot about his dangling pants. Arms flailing to regain his balance he found himself abruptly hoisted onto a passing float.

A feathered lizard with a man's face patted his back. "That's the Mardi Gras spirit, boy!" Somehow, Louise too was now on the float, flinging beads with great gusto. "Cher, any friend of the sweet Louise can be in my krewe any day, heathen or not."

Ping gazed in wonder at the warm, dark blush in his beloved's face. Her brown skin and curly hair still made his heart beat in strange rhythms. Once again he felt like a commoner in the presence of regal grace. Louise then bared her breasts and laughed. "Who cares about a li'l thing like a belly! Woopee!" This too was why he loved her.

☯

The thick walls of the small café held back most of the sounds of boisterous fun, thus making conversation once again possible. "So this is where you grew up, this New Orleans?" Ping swirled the wine in his glass noting the play of candle light on Louise's face through the red liquid.

Louise's eyes had gone dreamy with the haze of memory. "After Mamma and Daddy died I came here to live with Grand-mama Laveau.  She was a Big Voodoo Queen around here back then and I was treated like princess.  They was always house zombies to do the work and bodyguard me when I went out—They were kinda creepy and sad at the same time."

Ping smiled and made a mental note, *what is a zombie?*

He took another bite of his alligator gumbo and wondered what breed of chicken an alligator was—at least it tasted like chicken.  "Are voodoo coronations always held during the madness of Mardi Gras?  Most kings prefer to have all of the adoring, and fawning of a ceremonial crowning focused upon their own majestic selves."

Marie stirred her gumbo lazily.  "What do you know about kings and coronations?  They got themselves an emperor over there in China, don't they?  You are the light in my heart, Ping, but I don't see you getting' a whole lot of royal invites."

"Truly, I have only been to one such majestic function— the crowning of the king of the Yetis, but I was unfortunately betrothed to the king's daughter at the time.  It was all rather harrowing but I did have a very good seat from which to view the festivities."  Ping offered with a shrug.

Marie made her own mental note, *what the hell is a Yeti?*

"Well, around here, most everybody declares a truce during the holiday so not as many folks be killin' each other.  See, the thing is, it ain't always real apparent who is next in line when an old king dies.  A king don't usually get married to just one gal so there can be a whole lot of heirs runnin' around."  Louise made a dainty hiccup and took another sip of wine.  "So the voodoo queen chooses the new king but they don't get hitched or anything, it's all about the title.  Now, my Grand-mama Marie died just before that ol' coyote man snatched me and she left the throne empty.  I got lots of aunties and most of them claim to be the new queen but nobody's real sure and to make matters worse they are all named Marie.  It's confusing"

Ping balanced his spoon on one finger.  "This is where the matter confuses my own humble brain.  You are not the queen—you do not wish to be the queen and you are not highly educated in this voodoo religion which goes hand in hand with Catholic religion somehow.  So why exactly is your beautiful presence required at all for these august proceedings?"

Marie rolled her eyes and scooped up a mouthful of gumbo.  "I am the compromise!  My daddy was the only son of Marie Laveau and I am his only daughter so I have to choose a king and then he will choose a new queen and we can be shed of this whole mess.  Everybody seems convinced that I got me some big time juju talents so I got nominated and elected without anyone consulting me.  Grand-mama was always so good to me that I figure I owe her this.  The last thing she wanted was a big ol' blood-bath."

Ping threw his spoon into the air and watched it twirl as he digested the gumbo and their situation.  The spoon never came back to him.  It was abruptly snatched in mid-flight by a giant black fist.  "Louise Laveau, granddaughter of the last true Big Queen, you will come with me to serve at the pleasure Daddy DeKill, lord of the Krewe Macabre—or we kill you here.  Your choice."

Ping spun in his chair to see five large black men, heads shaven and wearing demon masks of purple, green and gold.  They were draped in glittering beads and chains of small metal skulls.  Their demeanor was most unfriendly.  Ping, not a fighter by nature but a natural born acrobat since birth whose skills had been honed by his time in a traveling circus, was already in motion.

He hopped onto his chair and did a perfect back-flip into his would be assailants.  He landed, each of his black-slippered feet finding a perch on the head one of the men.  Ping then thrust his feet out into a perfect split.  This forced the two heads underneath him violently into the two cohorts who closely flanked them.  They all dropped like slaughtered oxen with Ping atop them.  Immediately Ping repeated his back-flip barely clearing the top of the masked man who had first spoken.  He landed lightly atop the table barely sloshing a drop of either his or Louise's dinners.

"Run Louise.  I shall attempt to instruct this masked lout in the finer points of etiquette."  Ping stood atop the table, crouched only slightly, yet his eyes were even with man in the mask. *Most disconcerting.* He waved his hands in intricate patterns as he had seen fighters in his country do. He hoped this would look more menacing than ridiculous.

Ping never saw the enormous fist that sent him flying across the café. From his vantage point amid scattered chairs and tables, he did note Louise as she screamed curses and pummeled the masked demon who carried her away tucked under one enormous arm. This he noted but was unable to act upon as his eyes rolled back into their sockets.

☯

The young would-be hero awakened to the smell of vomit and the heaving sounds of someone unaccustomed to New Orleans caliber merry-making. He sat up, gingerly touching his nose. *Something about back alleys everywhere bear a remarkable resemblance.* This was the thought that skittered across Ping's tentative consciousness. By the level of muted hubbub he was sure he was still somewhere in the French Quarter of New Orleans but the city was a labyrinth of back alleys and courtyards and he was a bewildered rat, not seeking cheese but his lost Louise. Where would he even start?

He rose to the sound of solitary set of hands clapping slowly. "That was quite a pretty show you put on there, man of China, but I think you gotta work on the ending if you don't want your audience snatched off like that." A deep voice came out of the shadows followed by the gaunt figure of a man in a tattered tailcoat and top hat. "That little girl, she was my responsibility long before you set eyes on her. It does look like we are both damned sorry as defenders of Louise. I let that bastard, Coyote, take her all those years ago and now you lost her to the Krewe Macabre." The man tipped his hat, bowed and vanished.

Ping almost fell over as the same voice whispered from behind him. "I ain't got the same power in this world as I used to." Ping whirled but there was only the whisper. "I once promised a queen I'd see after whoever she passed her juju on to, but I am old and ragged and I failed." A skull wearing a top hat shimmered in the air for a moment and was gone. "Yeah, I failed but maybe you don't have to." A pouch appeared on the ground at Ping's feet. "You follow that there gris-gris and maybe we both still got a small shot at redemption."

Ping stuttered, "M-m-may I know your name, oh ancient and faded dread spirit?"

The distant noise of revelry hushed as a final whisper came. "You just tell that sweet girl that her ol' uncle Samedi ain't dead yet."

Slowly, carefully, Ping lowered himself to a cross-legged squat and poured the contents of the pouch onto the ground. His lip curled at the bloody chicken head and two severed poultry feet. But, lying there with them was a large coin on a chain. On one side was a skull and on the reverse were the Chinese characters that made up his name. This he slipped into his pocket. And, there was a crude doll dressed in silk, with seeds for eyes set at a slant on its yellowish face. It was as though the doll was meant to be an effigy of Ping. This too he slipped into a pocket.

Presently the ground began to tremble like a small San Francisco earthquake. The chicken feet danced around as though the bird still lived. Presently the head lifted above the feet and a whole chicken materialized before him. Instead of a cackle, the bird let out a hollow laugh and scampered off.

Ping blinked hard to make sure he was awake before he jumped to his feet and gave chase to this gris-gris chicken. Alligator and now gris-gris—he wondered what other breeds of chicken New Orleans had to offer.

☯

Chasing a re-animated chicken through Mardi Gras was even more of a challenge than Ping could have imagined. Many times the bird would dodge between dancing legs and flowing skirts forcing Ping into compromising positions. He quickly became accustomed the frequent slaps and constant cursing. The only apology he offered was a curt bow. Less than that would have been unseemly. Once, a reveler grabbed the chicken and tossed it high into the air. Amid flapping wings and flying feathers it was caught and thrown back into the air. This became a game for the crowd and soon the bird was blocks away.

Ping was not a tall man and so his quarry was quickly lost in the distance. Now he cursed—loudly and in several Chinese dialects. Shoulders slumped he elbowed his way to the crowd's edge. He had never felt so unworthy. He lurched to a nearby wall to beat his fist upon it and sob. For five minutes he enjoyed this unparalleled opportunity for a pity party, before something landed on his head. A single sharp chicken toe tapped out an impatient tattoo on his grieving skull before the bird jumped down and fled into an alley. Ping was in hot pursuit, taking only long enough to wipe his nose on a silken sleeve.

The French Quarter was a rabbit warren of anonymous walls, windows, narrow alleyways and wrought iron. There were people in the streets but the crunching press of humanity had thinned as the distance from the parades increased. In seeming frustration with the blind alleys and broken cobblestones the chicken flapped its way up a wall and onto a roof. Ping followed. He was an excellent climber.

He could not help but notice the marked difference between the nondescript public exteriors of buildings and the lush, elaborate courtyards that lay hidden in their interiors. During Mardi Gras the people wore masks but the city itself wore a mask all the year to hide its true face to strangers. Chicken and man ran as if a demon pursued them. They leapt over chimneys, scrabbled over steep pitches of roof and danced through crumbling, loosened tiles. They hurdled from one roof to the next never pausing to gauge distance or danger.

Where the buildings ended, a white, graveyard city began. Louise had told him how bodies of the New Orleans dead had to be buried above ground in ornate tombs of polished stone. The waterline would just push a casket from six feet down up to the surface in no time—the smell was not pleasant when that happened. Here the running was faster and the silence was oppressive. Ping raced on though his ribs stung like fire grates. His clothing and thin slippers were in tatters and the moon provided just enough light to dodge the white homes of the dead. Still, he vowed the chicken would not lose him again.

The grave city ended rather more abruptly than seemed right and he found himself wading through knee deep fetid water. Ahead he saw trees draped in Spanish moss and shifting darkness. A quick glance over his shoulder only revealed more of the same with no sign of the marble tombs he had just traversed. A deep breath turned into a ragged cry of anguish. He saw the chicken in the distance and spat a mouthful of fury in its direction. There was no turning back now.

His quarry somehow pranced lightly across the still, fetid waters of the bayou but Ping could only plunge on through a tide that was often up to his waist. He said a quick prayer to any god that might be listening that the waters would grow no higher. Once he got caught by a patch of mud that aspired to the noble calling of quicksand. Try as he would he could gain no purchase to pull himself free. The chicken, of course, was no help at all. Though he felt no current, he did spy a large log, moving at a good speed, coming in his direction. He grabbed at its rough bark as it sailed past and was soon pulled free.  He let the log carry him some distance before he noticed this log had legs and a tail. It seemed prudent to take his leave of the log at that point. He made a mental note to keep a watch for whatever sort of tree this log might have fallen from.

The swamp played a symphony of its own making made up of strange bird calls and sighing branches, but one sound soon dominated all others. It was a plaintive, high, wordless song that drifted along the thin fog which had become universal and oppressive. The chicken scampered in the direction of the song so Ping followed.

There was dry ground beneath his feet now and he felt he could go no further without a minute's rest. He let his sore, scratched and battered body crumple to the grass where he lay on his back, breathing hard. Once his lungs were working normally again he opened his eyes and beheld the gnarled tree branch above him. Perched on the branch sat the chicken and the source of the song. A rangy and ragged man sat there playing a fiddle. His bow strokes were long and quavered with sadness as his unseeing eyes scanned the heavens with a longing that made Ping's breath catch once again.

"Friend," Ping exclaimed, "O' poet prince of unspeakable melancholy, I seek Louise, granddaughter of a queen and owner of my deepest longings. I follow that chicken seated to your left and it has led me to you. Please, will you speak?"

The fiddler stopped in mid-note and pointed his fraying

bow out toward the open water. The fog parted and Ping saw a shallow draft boat being poled their way by a figure draped in a gray funeral shroud. "Am I to go with this spectral ferryman? Is that your instruction?" Ping was on his feet once again to get a better view of the approaching apparition." His tiredness began to manifest itself as anger. "It is not that I do not appreciate the theatricality of this scenario, I myself often cultivate a flair for the dramatic, but would a simple answer be too much to ask?"

The unseeing musician laughed and the chicken joined in. That was the last straw. "I am Chin Song Ping, son of celestial parents and defeater of demi-gods. I have released my share of ghosts from bondage and dueled with poetry spouting monsters. I have dined with Yeti royalty and beaten every manner of being, human, and otherwise, at games of chance. I am not to be trifled with and demand some respect!" Then, with a sense of comic timing that could only be attributed to divine intervention, Ping's britches fell around his ankles for the second time that night.

"Please?" he added weakly.

The fog reminded Ping of San Francisco—he hated San Francisco. Fog was the only thing he saw from the bow of the boat as it slid past silent shadows of swaying giants. The fiddle man had eventually spoken to him after he fell out of the tree in a fit of hysterical guffaws. He told Ping that the ferryman would take him to someone who would give him the means to find Louise. Furthermore he cautioned Ping not to converse with the boat's pilot as they would be traveling through treacherous channels and he must not be distracted. The fiddler kept the chicken.

The boat reached its destination with a thud. A skeletal hand reached out from the shroud in a gesture that Ping knew well—time to pay the ferryman. He reached into his pocket and produced the coin on the chain that had come with the gris-gris chicken. The ghostly figure studied it for a moment and shook its head. Ping shrugged and produced the gold piece he always kept hidden on his person for emergencies. This seemed to qualify. "This is a twenty dollar coin so I should have change coming back to me."

The hand took it greedily and disappeared back under the shroud. No move was made to make change. A rumble of words issued forth. "You are in the land of the dead. Stay to the path. Tourists are not welcome here."

Ping gulped back something with an acid taste and bowed. "Your service was most excellent, good sir, and I hope you remember my generosity when next we meet." The boat and pilot faded into the fog.

The path was well marked and paved with what Ping assumed were good intentions. His destination was equally clear. A dead woman sat serenely in a brocade chair while another woman, darker in complexion, shaped her long hair into improbable loops and whorls.

Ping cleared his throat. "Pardon my intrusion ladies, but I am Chin Song Ping, a humble seeker of knowledge upon these dread shores."

The darker woman tapped the shoulder of her client who promptly shuffled off into the gloom. "C,mon up here, cher, and let Mamma Marie take a look at you." The hairdresser patted the chair seat.

A grin tugged at his mouth as he sat. "You are Marie Laveau, the great and revered Voodoo Queen?" He knew this to be true, though why she played this servant role was a mystery. "Louise, your granddaughter, is in grave danger and I must save her. I believe that this is why I am here."

"Darlin', you look a fright and it's been way too long since your last haircut." Ping had long ago desisted from the prevalent style of long hair tied into a queue and a shaven head. He wore a small, discreet queue but had otherwise gone with a more western look. "Back when I was alive I was the most sought after hairdresser in all Louisiana. I was the best and those swells told me all their secrets as I made them beautiful— knowledge is power, sweetie and I had power. Plus, the job of bein' a queen don't pay as well as most folks think."

Ping sat speechless as Marie's scissors chirped about his head like an ecstatic cricket. "As for Louise needing to be rescued, that's very sweet, but she is a big girl now and has to learn who she is." Marie sighed, "Men almost never see power in women and when they do they run away like a hungry bear had smelled honey on their privates."

Ping turned his head to disagree but strong fingers set him facing forward once again.

"I think you might just be an exception to the rule, so I brought you out here to meet you. Don't worry, you have a role to play in this upcoming shindig but you can't go there looking like a scarecrow in his pajamas." Ping glanced down to see that his tattered clothing had been replaced with the elegant finery of a western style tuxedo. "Now, I never took the time to explain to my granddaughter how powerful she was—that was an oversight on my part—so when the time comes you have to convince her of what she is capable of. That's simple enough, right?" She handed him a mirror as she brushed at his shoulders. He did look rather dashing if he said so himself. She spun him around and stuck out her hand in the same gesture as the ferryman. "Ain't nothin' free in life or death and I am a professional stylist," she said.

Ping felt in his new pocket and, sure enough, there was the coin and chain. Marie took it from him and raised it high in a blessing before she kissed it and placed it around his neck. "Now you are ready for the party. Have fun."

The bottom dropped from Ping's chair and he plunged into a dark, bottomless abyss. His scream was most dignified, all things considered.

☯

English is a strange language. Though Ping spoke perfect English, thanks to a magical upgrade, he was always frustrated by the number of words that had multiple meanings. One could row a boat or plant a row of corn. One might use pitch to repair the roof or pitch a ball to a dog. So naturally when Louise had mentioned going to a ball, he had assumed a sporting event.

His fall into black nothingness had been terrifying at first but the length of the plunge soon leeched away the novelty and Ping fell asleep. A nudge to his shoulder had awakened him—a nicely turned-out waiter was offering him champagne. Women in finery of every description whirled past clinging to the arms of men dressed much as Ping was. A small orchestra played the jaunty music that Ping had learned to think of as a waltz—Louise loved to waltz.

In the middle of the room was a raised stage with an ornate throne. Seated on the throne was a mean-looking black man in a tall top hat, smoking a very large cigar. He was not particularly large or powerful looking, but his eyes were not eyes to be messed with. At his side was a wooden staff topped with feathers and a silver skull. Ping downed his champagne in a gulp and started a battle march straight for the throne.

Before he had managed three steps, a tug on his arm swept him into the embrace of one of the dancers. His new partner wore a blood-red tuxedo and a diamond-studded top hat. Clutched tightly between his teeth was a stogie cigar that had been chewed quite thoroughly. Indeed, all his teeth shone in a grin that was disconcerting, for a grin is the natural expression of a skull.

"Uncle Samedi?" Ping blurted out in delight. "You seem much improved from when last I saw you."

"Well thanks, Cher. These soirees always pick me up a bit." The skull explained around the stogie. "This here coronation is a formal affair, though, so I must insist on my official title of baron."

Ping bowed his head slightly, "I meant no disrespect. I am unused to skeletal royalty."

"Understandable," Somehow Ping knew that the Baron's empty eye socket had winked at him. "This here is the grand ball of the Krewe Macabre. They are usually sort of a two-bit outfit but since they kidnapped Louise they were able to force all the other crown contenders to show up here." The baron shook his head so hard his hat almost fell off. "DeKill's daddy, the last real Big King, Papa Midnight, would never condone such hijinx."

Ping felt his body tipped back almost to the floor—his first dip as a dipee. "You are a damned fine dancer for a foreigner!" The baron raised him up and gave him a twirl.

"Word is that if all his half-brothers don't agree to have Louise crown him, he will just kill her and let the machetes decide the matter." Samedi blew a wreath of smoke that changed into an arrow pointing toward a draped doorway guarded by two dead-eyed gentlemen. "That is where she is being held, two zombies at the door and a bunch more inside." He pulled an ornate watch from his pocket. "Almost midnight, good time for things to happen, so get to hero-ing." The baron suddenly vanished as Ping finished yet another twirl.

Daddy DeKill stood up from his central perch and banged his staff three times on the platform. The music stopped abruptly and the choreography broke up into a mob of anxious, random movement. DeKill's high, nasal voice rang out, "New Orleans has gone without a Big King for too long!" The crowd murmured loudly for a moment before he pounded his staff again, "We all agreed to bring in a king-maker so here she is." The curtains parted and a small army of zombies shuffled out with Louise held high in a kicking frog-march. She was dressed in an elegant yellow gown with a matching scarf crammed into her mouth. They hefted her onto the stage with DeKill. "The doors are all chained shut, so make no mistake, either I leave this room as Big King," each zombie produced a glistening blade and raised it above his head. "Or this city gets a ball it will never forget."

Ping felt a little dizzy—it had been a strange evening. He surveyed the room to decide which of his skill sets he might best employ in this situation. As an acrobat he might tumble his way through the crowd of onlookers and dazzle the zombies with his moves—though if they caught him they might rip his head off—they were quite muscular. As an actor he might bore them all to sleep with a long soliloquy—in Mandarin. As a gambler he might lure DeKill into a winner-take-all card game and win Louise's freedom—but he had no cards. Try as he might, he could not see how his prowess as a great lover might be brought to bear in this situation. Of course, he could always con them all into believing some outrageous premise which would end with them asking him to please take Louise and all their money and even the key to the city of New Orleans. That might work—Yes, BULLSHIT it would be!

Ping strode purposefully through the milling throng and nimbly hopped up onto the stage. He gently pushed a dumbfounded Daddy DeKill to one side and raised his coin amulet high above his head like a badge of office. "I am Chin Song Ping,

Sorcerer General of the International Association of Voodoo, Hoodoo and Mojo Practitioners! This building is surrounded with hopping ghosts who have hopped here on my command to put an end to this illegal coronation. Section fifty-two of sub-paragraph B clearly states that all contenders for mystical headgear must apply in person to the nearest Guru or Poobah on or before the last blood moon." Ping shook his finger sternly at DeKill. "No such application was ever made! If you wish to avoid penalties you may pay me at the door before I leave. Furthermore, it is my duty to take into custody," Ping took the gag from Louise's mouth—her eyes wide with amusement and disbelief. "This woman for the crime of...of..." He faltered.

Ping remembered how Marie had said Louise didn't need saving, she had true power—besides he could tell nobody was actually buying his bullshit. "For the crime of being too good for such idiocy as this." He hugged her tight and whispered in her ear. "Magic isn't about spells and ceremonies, it is the thing inside you—you are the power. Marie Laveau knew this, Coyote knew this when he took you and I know it with all my heart. Now you must believe it for yourself. Save everyone, my love."

At a sharp command from DeKill, strong, cold zombie hands pulled Ping away and lifted him for all to see. "This foreign devil has desecrated this gathering and I'm almost glad because now y'all get to see a demonstration of my will in action. Rip that Chinaman to pieces!!!"

Ping screamed his pain and anger as he felt the awful tug at his limbs.

"STOP!" Louise's voice rang out with an authority he had never heard before. Immediately he felt the zombie hands release him and he tumbled to the floor.

A deep shade of purple engorged DeKill's neck and face as he rounded to confront the woman who had dared defy him. "You little whore. I ought to..."

"SHUT UP!"

DeKill slumped to the ground. He grabbed desperately at his collar gasping for air. Louise stoically stepped over the writhing would-be king.

"When Papa Midnight died a while back," Louise's gaze

slowly scanned the crowd, "he didn't see fit to name an heir. When Marie Laveau passed, she followed his example." She looked into Ping's eyes and smiled. "Grand-mama Laveau never taught me a lot about voodoo but one thing I know is that it is a teaching of joy and celebration. It is a way to make our way through hard times together. What it ain't about is lordin' over each other. The time of masters and slaves is over."

She made a beckoning sign to Ping and the zombies lifted him back onto the stage. "Y'all followed Marie's wisdom while she was alive and I believe that I need to follow her last bit of wisdom now. I, the duly chosen king-maker, declare that there will be no more Big Kings or Big Queens. There was a war fought to give us our freedom but it ain't worth shit if we don't take responsibility for ourselves." She looked at the zombies who stood motionless. "And stop turnin' all these poor men into zombies. This ain't Haiti or Africa and it's a little embarrassing in this day and age."

Without another word she took Ping's hand and walked toward the door. As nervous members of the Krewe Macabre rushed to unshackle the portals, a voice came from the crowd. "What should we do with DeKill?"

Louise rubbed her forehead. "I am going to find me some beignets to feed to this sweet man of mine and then take him to bed for a week or so. I don't give a damn what you do with that fool."

At the door, Ping turned to the on-looking stunned faces and gave a deep bow followed with a one fingered gesture that he had come to regard as the epitome of the American attitude. They left and did not look back.

☯

Mardi Gras ended without further mishap. Ping and Louise enjoyed some of it from the relative privacy of their balcony. They talked about the mysteries of the Universe and agreed that whatever gifts she might possess were best used sparingly and only in the pursuit of joy. No one liked a show-off. On their last night in New Orleans, Louise dreamt of Marie Laveau. The next morning they visited the marble city of the dead and the Tomb of the last Big Queen of Voodoo.

Ping had cut a lock of his own hair and tied it around the

doll which was the last item from the gris-gris pouch—he laid it at her tomb door. Louise had made a fetish of her own and put it beside Ping's.

She held her swollen belly with tender, interlaced fingers. "I worry sometimes that the life we been leading might catch up to us one of these days—or worse yet, our baby."

Ping sighed, "I have no fear for our offspring with such a mother as you to protect them, but perhaps it is time to settle down and be good Americans. There is a newly completed bridge in the fair city of Brooklyn. I know a printer in St. Louis who can make us some very good, authentic looking bills of sale and there are many rich patrons who might love to possess a bridge of their own."

Louise let herself be helped into their waiting carriage. "Sounds interesting—tell me more."

"Hot damn, your grandma must have been a four slice toaster back then!" Private Winston was blinking hard to fight off the cold tiredness that had slowly hit each man in his turn. It had to be four A.M. but an equal dose of fear and amusement kept them awake. They had made a silent pact not to be killed in their sleep if it came to that.

"Kid, you are so lucky to still have both your grandparents. Mine died before I was born and I always wanted someone to tell me stuff my mom and dad would have blushed at." The sergeant took out his last cigarette and broke it in half—he gave one half to Tommy and the other to Corporal Russ. "Christ, if I didn't have this here bum leg I'd be stomping my feet to get warm about now.

Winston nodded, "Lousy Germans didn't even leave us anything to burn except a couple of lousy chairs and no kindling."

Duke stuck his hands under his arms and stomped around the room. "Sarge, if it makes you feel any better, stomping doesn't really help much. Heck, maybe we should set fire to this whole danged place. At least we'd die warm."

"Use your head, Private. You are wearing government issued clothing and boots and those bandages are government issue. Even you are a GI and that stands for government issue. You could get yourself in big trouble if you were to willfully destroy government property, right, Sarge?" Russ cocked his head toward where he knew Sergeant Cole was seated.

"Oh yeah," he replied. "Just because you're dead doesn't mean they won't court martial you. Why, your burnt, dead corpse could wind up in Leavenworth for the duration. How would your mother feel about that?"

Duke came back to the circle and plopped down on the floor. "Well then, I say Tommy needs to tell us another story."

"Sure. Why not." Tommy blew into his hands. "I have one that has presidents and dragons and even romance, well sort of. You've all heard about the Great San Francisco earthquake and fire"

"Mrs. O'Leary's cow, right?" Duke chimed in.

"Different fire." Tommy continued. "When I was a kid I had to write a paper about that in school and I made the mistake of telling Grandfather Ping and he told me the "real story". I got an F on that paper but I've never forgotten the story he told me..."

## CHIN SONG PING AND THE DRAGON MERCHANTS
### SAN FRANCISCO: 1906

Ping ducked as the hatchet whirled out of the fog embedding itself into a ragged playbill for a theater that had burned down the year before. Fog didn't really do justice to the heavy, gray atmosphere that covered the land, making walking a dangerous activity and running a sure recipe for disaster. Despite this fact, Ping ran headlong into the ubiquitous gray swirl—and ran smack into a wall. He staggered for a moment but his head was cleared wonderfully by the knife-wielding maniac that appeared in his path. Dropping to the ground, he slid neatly through the maniac's widespread legs on a loose layer of wet garbage and slime, bowling the ruffian over in the process. Behind him voices screamed curses, muffled somewhat by the atmosphere. Tonight the fog was so thick one might be tempted to call it a heavy drizzle though the constituent droplets seemed to defy the dictates of gravity, hovering as black pepper would in a soup. And it was cold! He should have listened to Louise and packed his woolen coat. A thermometer was useless to describe the numbing cold that penetrated into the bone as a result of the swirling miasma freezing the soul more than ice possibly could. As another hatchet sliced past his left ear, severing the queue Ping had worn his whole life, two thoughts came into his mind. One was, 'I was getting tired of wearing that ponytail anyway.' The other was, 'God, how I hate San Francisco!'

Ping jumped up onto a box that had materialized before him, launching himself into the air where he hoped he might find a friendly fire escape, but this was Chinatown, where one rarely found such luxuries. What his hands found instead was a clothesline. Suddenly his face met with wet undergarments stained in places that he found entirely unsettling. Ping disliked Chinatown even more than San Francisco proper. He used his momentum to propel him in an arc around the line, hurtling him far down the alley where he landed, rolling with the impact. How many years since his career as an aspiring acrobat had been cut tragically short by a slight indiscretion with the master acrobat's wife? But this was neither the time nor place to indulge in pleasant nostalgia.

Over long years, Chinatown had been built haphazardly. It was a wooden labyrinth of false fronts and secret passageways leading to hidden dens of iniquity that lured the depraved, no matter their skin color. It was a maze that had Ping thoroughly lost. If only he had a moment to sit, collect his thoughts, and get his bearings. 'Most unlikely,' he thought. Behind him, he heard the sound of one of his pursuers tripping over the box he had used as a springboard. As a knife whistled through the air, ventilating his jacket, he felt a rumbling beneath his feet and heard the insistent clang of bells in the distance. In San Francisco that meant only one thing, a cable car!

Perhaps he could survive this night after all.

He burst onto a busy avenue populated by a colorful array of humanity dressed in gaudy silk, ragged canvas and dapper, if unimaginative, western suits and dresses. This many whites had to mean that he wasn't far from the Stockton Cable Car line. So, he ran through the brightly lit fog, jumping over displays of fruit and vegetables, pushing through tourists and residents alike in a mad dash for the safety of the moving fortress on rails that he heard ahead.

Just as he thought his lungs might burst into flames, he saw the wooden and iron vehicle pulling away from its stop, heading for a steep descent. In one last desperate burst, he flung himself at the cable car and just managed to grasp an iron pole as the vehicle picked up speed. Swinging one foot onto the running board, he hollered "Duck!!"

A hail of hatchets and knives dug into seats and running board. Fortunately, the passengers were few and nimble, so there were no casualties. The gripman deftly dodged a small hatchet while urging the car on its way. The conductor emerged from the cabin, plucking various sharp implements from wooden panels.

He tossed them into the street with a certain jaded disdain as he made his way to Ping.

"That'll be two bits, pal," he said very matter-of-factly.

Ping reached into his pocket and retrieved a twenty dollar gold piece, his good luck charm. "I regret sir that this gaudy coin is all I have at the moment. Perhaps I might persuade you to accept it as an inducement to ignore the next several stops normally scheduled for your most noble vehicle."

The gripman and the conductor exchanged a look. They took judicious note of the sharp instruments still embedded in the seats and walls. They also assessed the group of angry men who had taken pursuit of the vehicle. After due consideration the conductor took the coin and winked at the gripman. "Enjoy your ride, sir," he said as he motioned Ping to take his seat.

☯

The hike from the end of the Stockton line to a rather seedy looking bar on the so-called Barbary Coast had left Ping feeling stiff and morose. Pulling off his left shoe as he sat down, he extracted a five-dollar bill squirreled away for just such an emergency. The smell of the bill was somewhat unpleasant, but in such surroundings the bartender barely noticed. Chinese were not served at many Barbary Coast establishments, however the Limping Dutchman had never observed such niceties. Four drinks later, Ping was sobbing softly as a burly man with a bristly mustache sat down loudly beside him.

"Barkeep!" The man roared, "Whiskey—your finest—and another round for my sorrowful friend here!"

Ping turned to look at the man, one eye drooping slightly. "Sir, you are a gentleman of great gentle…osity." He shook his head to sort the wool that had gathered within. "You have a look of intelligence about you. May this humble one ask an opinion about a dilemma in which he finds himself?"

The man laughed heartily and slapped him on the back. "Lad, I doubt many would agree about my intelligence these days but all my mental resources are at your disposal for the next…" He looked at his pocket watch, "Five minutes and thirty-five seconds."

"My name is Chin Song Ping and I am a man who has

always placed a high esteem on my freedom, yet now I am to be married and thus shackled to a life of connubial servitude. I care greatly for my beloved, Louise, but I know not whether I'm ready for such a commitment. I am a coward!"

"Nonsense! You are a man in your prime and this marriage would be quite a blow to your routines and rhythms. Have you thought of merely living with this woman? I know that the oriental mind can be liberal toward such things." His mustache bristled even more and he adjusted the glasses, which perched birdlike on his nose.

"That was my very point!" Ping perked up at having found such an understanding soul. "For almost twenty-five years we have lived together happily, and I would not want to see us split asunder by something like marriage." The man sat open mouthed and staring. "If the strain of marriage were to prove too much for us to bear, whatever would become of our five children?" The man's elbow, which had supported his chin, slipped off the bar and might have caused a lesser being to fall off his stool.

"Five nights ago," Ping continued, "Louise's grandmother, a powerful voodoo priestess long dead, came to my love in her dreams and said we must marry, and very soon. Granny Loa dictated that Louise be wed in a beautiful white and lavender gown in a grove of blossoming cherry trees... or the world is doomed." Ping sighed and sipped at his drink. "Both Louise and myself are quite fond of this world... so here am I in this wretched city trying to find a suitable dress for the great occasion."

The man's eyes narrowed. "Sir, a woman entering her middle years will come up with many strange notions. Though I sympathize with your desire to accommodate the lady's wishes, I have grave doubts that the world will halt its tread should you not wed. Has the lady in question been experiencing hot flashes?"

"Ah, just so!" Ping nodded his head vigorously, "You and I, as sane men of the world, might find such a claim outlandish, but who would tremble at the faint threat of world's end when faced with the real and present fury of a woman contradicted?"

Ping and the man both upended their drinks. "Bowing to

fate's dictates I have searched the city for two days to find a white and lavender dress fine enough to be worthy of saving the world. An hour ago I spied such a dress in a shop window but before I could find my way in, the dress was sold and gone. I chased the buyers to Chinatown, following them through back alleys and hidden tunnels to implore them to have pity upon my plight. I thought I had lost them when I heard music through a thin wall. I noticed light coming through a crack and endeavored to peek in. There, much to my surprise, I saw Pan Sai Kow—who I recognized as a chief of the Boo Hoo Dow Doy hatchet sons—dancing around, admiring himself in a mirror while wearing the dress I sought for Louise. In my shock I crashed through the flimsy wall, startling the hatchet chief. He quickly hopped out of the dress and called for his men to kill me for defiling his privacy. I managed to escape but am now plagued by the feeling that this might be an inauspicious sign. What do you think?"

Before the man could speak, six aged Chinese gentlemen dressed in stark black western suits flooded through the saloon door. "Mr. President, you will come with us!"

Ping squinted one eye at the mustached man who had jumped to his feet and assumed a boxer's pose. He leapt to his feet beside the embattled president and assumed a similar pose, though he had never boxed anyone in his life. "Mr. President Teddy Roosevelt, forgive this lowly one for not recognizing your grand self earlier. You seem much shorter when perched atop a bar stool."

Roosevelt grinned fiercely, "Bully for you! Heathen you might be, but I thank you for standing with me." Ping gulped as several more Chinese pushed their way into the room—young men, tall and burly, with wicked smiles and sharpened blades at the ready.

"Perhaps this would be a propitious time to summon your Secret Service legions? I have read that such men were always around you."

"I had to ditch them. They would have insisted I not come here to personally meet an informant. Damned nuisance sometimes, being the President!" T.R. ducked a heavy-handed blow and jabbed his opponent in the solar plexus as Ping hopped onto the bar behind him to escape a slash from a curved knife. Leaping out to a rather shabby looking chandelier he swung through the goon squad and landed in the midst of the aged gentlemen. His thought was to use one of these six as a hostage and secure safe exit for himself and the president.

He grabbed a particularly frail looking old man by the throat, "I have no wish to harm you but if you do not stop this I will snap your neck like a twig in winter." The old man twisted and broke his hold so quickly and easily that Ping almost cried out in alarm. Suddenly, he felt himself flying through the air, thinking, not for the first time, "Am I the only wretch from China who does not know martial arts?" He crashed into the mirror over the bar and felt himself blacking out as soon as he hit the floor. The last thing he heard before oblivion was Teddy Roosevelt bellowing, "Take that, you Celestial son of a bitch!" He could not recall if he had voted for the fellow or not.

☯

Ping awoke spluttering through the water splashing into his mouth and nose. A hand yanked him upright by his newly shortened hair and snarled. "Where is the president, you slant-eyed runt?"

Over the years, Ping had learned to ignore racial epithets as products of ignorance and unwarranted arrogance. He would not tolerate such remarks to his children or wife—his modest wealth and status did afford some measure of dignity—but when directed at himself he was willing to be more philosophical. "Pardon my ignorance in this matter, but I seem to have been on another plane of consciousness when that most worthy gentleman left these premises." His inquisitor backhanded him, leaving Ping to spit out the blood pooling in his mouth.

This man was tall and muscular, dressed blandly and had obviously eaten large amounts of garlic with his evening meal. "We have reports that the president was seen being dragged from this bar by a bunch of Chinese, and you're Chinese. So where is the president?" He let Ping loose and pulled out a badge which said, 'Secret Service.' "I can make matters very unpleasant for you if you don't start cooperating!"

Ping straightened his clothing and pulled back his disheveled hair, "Ah, when last I saw Mr. President Teddy Roosevelt,

I was attempting to do the job you are paid for!" A dangerous twinkle formed in the agent's eye. "Please do not take my
word, you need but ask the worthy keeper of this bar. Surely he
saw it all." The man let out a snort and jerked his thumb down
the bar where another man in an apron lay in a pool of blood
with a hatchet imbedded in his skull.

"He's not talking so good right this minute. So that leaves
you as our only lead." Two more nondescript men came behind
the bar and Ping could only assume that their scientific questioning techniques might include the brass knuckles one was
fitting on his hand.

Had he paused a moment to consider the alternatives, he
might have taken the beating and hoped for the best. Instead
he did a near perfect back flip over the wooden bar, landing
feet first on a table filled with half empty beer mugs. These he
kicked into the faces of the gawking Secret Service men and
was out the door before they could even react.

☯

Ping had already surmised that the six old men in black
suits had to be the heads of the six families which comprised
the Consolidated Chinese Benevolent Association, though why
they should kidnap the president was beyond him. This meant
a return to Chinatown and probably more hatchets, but the
honorable President Teddy was the only one who might clear
his name—and there was still the matter of the dress.

As the agents rushed past his hiding place, which consist-
ed of shadows and trash in a nearby alley, he made himself as
small and insignificant as possible and considered the problem
of disguise.

In China he had briefly been understudy to one of the
greatest actors in the land, Ooh Long, celebrated as the man of
one thousand and eighty-seven faces for his skill with makeup.
One night, half way through the comedic farce 'The Emperor's
Chicken' Ping finally made his stage debut when Ooh Long
complained of stomach pains. He was a hit with the audience
until interrupted by angry merchants demanding payment for a
long list of services rendered to one Ooh Long. Ping swore that
he was merely the understudy and quickly removed his makeup
to prove the fact. Sadly, it seemed that the unscrupulous actor

had disguised himself as Ping when running up his enormous bills. Young Ping barely escaped ten years labor in a mine by ducking under the stage and escaping in the leading lady's favorite yellow frock. Though that ended his promising career as a thespian, he had learned much about the craft.

Simplicity was always best. He had worn his best western-style suit for the shopping expedition. So first, he removed his cravat to tie his hair back into a pale ghost of his former queue. Next he ripped the silk lining out of his jacket and made a colorful, though ragged-looking, shirt of it. His white western shirt became an apron, which helped secure the lining in place. He kicked off his shoes in favor of a barefoot motif and used smudges of mud to create a credible mustache, beard and uni-brow. It was, at best, a ludicrous, eccentric outfit. In other words, he should blend in rather well in San Francisco.

At least he had a destination. The Benevolent Association boasted a veritable palace at the heart of Chinatown, a fortress some might say. Ping looked at the fog-shrouded hills rising in his path, the path to Chinatown. Among his many other grievances toward this city, the three dimensional nature of its geography surely ranked high right then. "I should have stayed at home and let the world end," he grumbled.

☯

If the alleyways of Chinatown were an inscrutable maze, then the rooftops were an ever-shifting minefield of loose wood, broken shingles and hidden holes. Ping, thankful for his months of training as a blindfolded tightrope walker, threaded his way onto ever-higher summits of treacherous footholds. The Benevolent Association headquarters was naturally the highest structure on the tallest hill in Chinatown, thus easily found even from this perspective. He thought to himself that he should always traverse Chinatown in this manner, the visibility was much clearer and the stench was almost bearable. To the southwest he saw a flash, as if it were lightning, but it seemed to come from the sea itself rather than overhead and there was no thunder which followed. Probably some new marvel being tested, electrical he shouldn't wonder. This new American century was only in its sixth year but seemed to show no sign of slowing down. Carriages without horses, men flying about like birds—Ping considered himself a liberal thinker but he sometimes wished all this science would slow down just enough for his brain to keep pace.

He came at last to a small skylight, situated over a tiny dark room. This would be the third story flush toilet, so highly touted in the Chinese newspapers a year ago, which was the pride of the Six Families. It was proclaimed as the ultimate symbol of how progressive Chinatown had become. Nimbly lowering himself, he felt one foot descend into wetness and prayed to a merciful deity that the thing had been recently flushed.

After drying his toes and smelling the towel, he eased open the door to find a hallway, silent and dark. Without a sound he made his way to the stairwell where he heard angry voices arguing below. Stairs were tricky. No matter how careful, one would always seem to find a squeaky board, so he opted for sliding down the banister. The voices seemed to emanate from behind a closed door with light leaking out from below. It felt terribly exposed, but he could see no alternative. Quietly, he cupped his hand to his ear and leaned in close to the wooden-paneled door.

"Kill him, I say!" a nasal voice whined, "This Roosevelt has made many enemies. Someone shot his predecessor. Maybe no one would notice if this one disappeared as well."

A dry voice hissed in reply. "You speak like an ass braying!" There was a sharp thumping sound. "If this president knew of our plans, how many more might also know? We were lucky we managed to intercept the traitor, Chang, before he could fully disclose what will happen this night. Otherwise, the Emperor's dreams of a new, progressive China would be destroyed forever and the Empress Dowager…" Ping heard the sounds of multiple expectorations hitting the floor, "…would keep our ancestral homeland trapped in a feudal cesspool to be abused like a cheap whore by the west. We must tread carefully."

A low rumbling voice added, "Roosevelt is a crusader. We are simply one more thing against which he can rail to proclaim himself a champion and defender of the people. His cities are overflowing and must be fed. The unfeeling industry that has grown up to meet this demand abuses its power, callous to the deaths and misery it also manufactures. He fights against tainted meat because that is the cause of the day. He merely sees another potential target in our endeavor."

Ping's blackened eyebrows knitted together as he whispered to himself, "Tainted meat?"

The rumbling man continued, "If we can convince him that what we offer is not tainted in any way, we may gain an ally where once we had an enemy."

There was a murmur of agreement. "Then we are decided. We shall tempt Roosevelt with a deal he can hardly refuse— and kill him if he does refuse."

Ping dropped to the floor at the sound of footsteps and started scrubbing as hard as he could with his apron/shirt. When the old men emerged, sure enough, they did not defile their dignity to take notice of a lowly servant. All six filed by him, followed by a burly bodyguard who gave Ping a perfunctory kick just on principle.

Confused but undaunted, Ping followed the others at a discrete distance to a sub-basement where he saw the President pacing like a cornered lion in a small cell. T.R. stopped cold in his tracks when he saw his captors. "I hope you fully realize the ramifications of your acts. This heinous behavior constitutes nothing less than an act of war!"

"Most honorable Mr. President Teddy Roosevelt," the whiney man stepped forward. "No doubt we were overly enthusiastic in our misguided efforts to secure a private audience, but rest assured we never meant for any harm to come to your august personage."

The rumbling man continued, "We would merely offer this great country, which we also love, a new dawn, a way to feed your masses, to repopulate your plains with something more wonderful and enduring than the buffalo at its prime."

The president stuck out his chin defiantly. "I have been informed already of the abominations you offer, sickly things that your country can hardly sustain. Now you would foist your rejects off on America—shameful, sir, shameful."

The old man rumbled in reply. "I humbly offer that you were misinformed. We have at this very moment, tethered off Mussel Rock, just south of the city, one magnificent male and four enthusiastic females. They were sedated with opiates during their journey here, but I have telephoned my people to revive the leviathans most expediently, so that you might see them for yourself. Imagine, these great beasts roaming free on the vast American prairies, breeding to become great herds. Cattle and swine would pale by comparison as a rich food source for a ravenous nation." Roosevelt relaxed somewhat but remained wary. "They are wild and savage beasts," the old man continued, "but easily subdued into docility by simple burnt opium. In the wild they are the preferred hunting game of emperors for over a thousand years."

Roosevelt's mustache twitched as his eyes twinkled with a far-away light. "Gadfry! I've always dreamed of bagging a dragon."

Ping almost choked on his tongue.

☯

Dragons had always held a special place of dread in Ping's mind. As a child, his mother's favorite threat at misbehavior was that she would summon a dragon to swoop down and bite his head right off his shoulders if he continued to act out in some unruly manner. Indeed, as he was usually unruly in one form or another, he spent his early years constantly looking over his shoulder for an imminent dragon attack. He was deeply relieved to discover, upon leaving home at the age of fourteen, that dragons were merely a fairy story to frighten children. They were a myth, although a powerful one. What village or city did not have a colorful cloth dragon wind sensuously down its streets at least once a year?

During his brief time as a seller of rare antiquities, he had managed to part a wealthy merchant from a sizeable bag of gold by simply convincing him that two polished marble balls were thousand-year-old dragon testicles.

Then here in America, there were tales of monstrous dragons fought by European knights. Why, Mexico even had a great, feathered serpent as a national symbol. And here were powerful men who calmly discussed the beasts as a given. The concept that real dragons might somehow be introduced to his adopted country was enough to send a chill through his bladder.

☯

Theodore Roosevelt was accustomed to riding in an automobile, and considered himself a brave man, but even he was unprepared for the driving abilities of the deep-voiced old man called Chu Chu Chang. Chang drove at breakneck speeds of up to forty miles an hour over fog slick roads paved with cobblestones, or not at all. The vehicle barreled through streets that had grown up with little sense of planning or safety. Visibility was almost nonexistent, even where the lamplights gave off their faint ghostly orange glow. Roosevelt was also gaining a new respect for the depth and passions of Chinese curses as Chang kept up a running commentary on the stupidity of pedestrians, wagons and other autos, which narrowly dodged his progress.

All six aged Chinese patriarchs and their burly bodyguard were also crammed into the auto, discouraging any hope of escape as effectively as the iron chains binding Roosevelt's hands and feet. His emotions were as torn as his shirt cuffs by the naked iron.

To set himself against such a magnificent beast with only his wits and a very large caliber rifle was the dream of any red-blooded sportsman... On the other hand, did he want to be responsible for introducing such monsters into the open plains of America? He could see where ravaging behemoths might be a hindrance to potential settlement or mining interests. Also, he could not help but wonder if dragon meat were as nutritious and untainted as these gentlemen insisted, why China wasn't the best-fed nation on Earth. It was a puzzle that he felt inadequate to solving under present circumstances. Perhaps when they reached this Mussel Rock, and he could more clearly see the situation, he would evolve a bold and decisive plan of action—something Presidential, by God!

☯

Clinging tenaciously to the rear spare tire, Ping kept his eyes tightly shut, murmuring a long string of halfhearted prayers to every deity he had ever heard of. The thought kept running through his mind that Chicago was not so far away by rail and doubtlessly carried a much larger selection of fine wedding dresses.

As the auto screeched to a brief halt to allow a cable car the right of way, Ping opened his eyes and thought to slip away, allowing events to unfold as they would without his further interference. As he eased one foot to the street he glanced at the three men stalking along the sidewalk in the soft gaslight illumination, thinking that one looked very familiar. As he met the man's eyes, he realized that his disguise was not as good as he had hoped, for he saw instant recognition in the eyes of Pan Sai Kow, chief of the Boo Hoo Dow Doy hatchet sons. Ping lifted his foot just as the auto roared away; sparing him from the hatchet that had been aimed squarely at his fake uni-brow. This whole affair was becoming decidedly unpleasant.

☯

City streets eventually gave way to barely paved coastal trails boasting wild stretches of hairpin turns and sheer drops to jagged boulders. Once he saw a great spume of vomit from the passenger's side which he thought had a presidential cast to it. The roar of surf on stones was so loud, it blotted out the auto's engine and even the sharp voices of the old men as they argued and lectured. He had learned a few facts, though, during the earlier parts of the journey and was trying to make sense of them now.

Dragons were big. The male of the group that had been brought to these shores was said to be a quarter-mile long and twice as large around as a grain silo. Long centuries of inactivity had grown them to proportions never imagined in the old tales.

Dragons were strong. A tale was told of a dragon who had a nightmare as it slept its opium-induced slumber and had taken to twitching its tail. This had removed the top of a small hill, as well as killing three hundred attendants whose organs were turned to mush by the great vibrations produced as the tail hit the ground. In nearby Tibet, temple gongs rang out though no hand had struck them. This story was not repeated in English for Roosevelt.

Dragons could fly. They were filled with thousands of gas bladders, which allowed them to hover just off the ground, making the monsters as easily maneuvered as soap bubbles—or so it was said. Hundreds of thousands of feathered flaps served as wings that could propel the leviathans at great speeds, but only for short distances. The wings were kept clipped and were only in use at feedings. Like great hovering cows, dragons ate grass.

Dragons breathed fire. The gas produced to allow them to fly was belched forth occasionally and would be ignited should a dragon gnash its great stony teeth, eliciting a spark. This was a common occurrence, it seemed, as they dreamt their dragon dreams. It was the main cause of death among dragon attendants.

There were not many dragons left in the world. A thousand years before, the dragons had been subdued and domesticated, retained against the threat of invasion, but they had died for lack of activity. All except a few. Ten of the great beasts survived and grew to enormous size, kept secluded in a remote corner of the kingdom. They were a secret and ultimate symbol of the Emperor's power. When the west had made its great incursion from across the ocean, two dragons were awakened and sent to destroy the invaders while still at sea. Exploding shells from a gunboat made short work of China's defenders, turning the gas bladders into huge fireballs. China stood defenseless and jaded in their long, smug assumption of power. Ping had not seen his native land in over a quarter century but this saddened him and explained much about China's present standing in the world.

☯

Between the chill in his fingers and the icy hand which clutched at his stomach, Ping was again ready to abandon his quest when, all of a sudden, the automobile skidded to a sudden, gravel-plumed stop throwing the passengers forward and dislodging Ping from his perch. He was thrown to the side and was afraid of discovery until he saw what had made the driver stop so precipitously. From a small island, off to the right, there came a fireball, arcing through the night toward the auto. The doors opened, spilling out passengers scrambling madly for safety. Ping froze for only a second before he used the rear fender as a springboard to propel himself at the manacled form of the president. As the fireball hit the hood of the auto, Ping bore the president to the ground, covering him as best he could.

Shaking his head to clear it, Ping removed a pin from Teddy's lapel and made short work of the locks at his hands and feet.

It was amazing how much he remembered from his long ago affair with the great lock-pick, Zhing Zhoh. He hadn't had much occasion to use those skills since he had helped her steal a nobleman's great jade turtle yo-yo from a locked tower.

Ping helped the president to his feet and they saw the flaming, misshapen form of a man, which had fallen from the sky to destroy the auto's engine so thoroughly. That small island he had noted before was suddenly alive with flame and screaming which was heard even over the roar of the ocean. Roosevelt leaned heavily on his shoulder as they hobbled to the cliff edge along with Chu Chu Chan and his brethren. "Perhaps waking the brutes wasn't such a bully idea after all." Roosevelt offered as he looked out to sea.

They beheld a large steamship moored to the island, battered and burning, with four dragons circling overhead and spitting flames. Chan wailed out that the ship was the one that had brought the tethered giants from China. A fifth dragon, the largest, undoubtedly the male, lay huddled on the great rock island watching his harem wreak devastation. As they watched in disbelief, an American gunboat appeared over the horizon speeding to the rescue of the ocean liner.

Chan and the other old men waved their gnarled hands wildly, yelling at the top of their lungs for the gunboat to go away.

The president turned his head, squinting hard at Ping for the first time. His lips spread into a fierce grin. "Why, you're the fellow needing a dress to save the world!"

Back down the dirt road came the sound of screaming engines and savage war cries as two carloads of men brandishing hatchets flew over a hill, barreling toward the dazed group of Benevolent Family heads, their captive president and the bedraggled Ping. "Let me guess, this would be the cross-dressing hatchet fellow and a few of his friends." The president intoned.

Ping shrugged, "So it would seem. How did you know?"

Teddy flexed his fists and threw off his jacket to make ready for battle. "Seemed as reasonable a guess as anything else this night."

Over the hills to the east, the sun's first rays broke through the fog and brought the sound of a giant mosquito. A small flying machine buzzed in topping the hills, coming in low over the cars filled with hatchetmen forcing them off the road. One went flying off the cliff and the other into a boulder. Teddy laughed and pointed as the flying machine flew on toward the flaming island. "Ain't she a beauty?" The president waved at the pilot, who Ping recognized as the Secret Service man who was so fond of garlic. Ping deduced the man had probably managed to track down Mr. Teddy by simply flying around the city until he spotted them. Very scientific, if a bit late.

The commander in chief beamed with pride. "Had it made from some plans the Wright boys drew up for me. That's what brought me out here in the first place, to give her a test run and, by Gadfry, she's all I could have hoped for. I think I'll call her my Air Horse One!"

Ping thought that those elected to such a high office should be thoroughly and regularly examined to determine their continued sanity.

He pushed the president aside and ducked as the foot of an elderly man in black threatened to take his head off. As the foot sailed by, Ping launched his own foot squarely into the old man's groin. This was clearly not an honorable move, but it worked.

The flying machine had banked out over the ocean and was headed back toward them when the earth lurched. The huge form of the male dragon separated itself from the rocks of the island, to give chase to the machine. Everyone was thrown off their feet when, an instant later, the winged device sailed over them and an immense form crashed into the cliff-side below.

☯

Somehow, Pan Sai Kow, chief of the Boo Hoo Dow Doy hatchet sons, had managed to stagger forward through the car crash and the great earth movement. Such was his fury to destroy the outsider who had seen him indulge his enthusiasm for beautiful things—such as western women's dresses—he had barely noticed the pandemonium arrayed around him. Running and screaming, he saw Ping at last. There would be no escape this time. Kow pulled his largest hatchet from his belt and threw it straight at Ping's back.

☯

Ping stood at the cliff's edge shaking in terror. Up the side came a feathered face with a wide mouth and huge luminous eyes, not quite focused but clearly agitated. All strength fled Ping and he fell to his knees just as the eyes crested the cliff. From behind him, a large hatchet whirled past, sticking deep into one of the enormous orbs. Surely the shock more than the pain sent the dragon into a thrashing frenzy that flung men and battered autos flying into the air as the very earth moved once again.

From the island below, the coast guard gunboat let out with several rounds of large caliber gunfire. Four great fireballs lit up the still-shadowed shoreline, signaling the dazzling demise of the four female dragons.

The male halted his thrashing for just a moment and Ping could see the torment in the great eyes as the dragon launched himself into the air. Ping glanced behind him to see the hatchet chief raise another weapon.

Again, had he thought for a moment longer he might have taken his chances with a hatchet to the head, but instead he turned back and leaped as hard as he could over the cliff, grabbing a handful of feathers as the mighty creature propelled itself toward the falling ruins of San Francisco.

The air was crisp and biting as Ping clung for dear life. He had always supposed dragons to be scaly, perhaps slimy, but the creature was soft as a downy featherbed, providing innumerable hand and foot holds. So he climbed. After some progress he dared look ahead, just long enough to ascertain that he was indeed near the head of the thing for he saw what must be an ear. He looked to the earth below and saw devastation stretching to the horizon where minutes before a great city had sprawled. The dragon let fly a stream of flaming bile onto the city, causing Ping to cry out. He had never cared for San Francisco or Chinatown, but he had also never wished to see such devastation dealt to the city and its citizens.

If ever a living being had cause for terrible vengeance, surely it was this dragon. The old tales spoke of sages who could reason with dragons, moving them to pity for the plight of poor deluded mortals. Ping was no sage but he had to do something, so he crawled toward the great ear, hoping he could find words to stay the wrath of a force of nature.

Drawing himself close to the opening, he screamed at the top of his lungs. "Noble lord of the land and sky, this humble gnat seeks your benevolent notice!" Another rain of flames flew down from immense mouth, engulfing yet another part of the city. Ping closed his eyes and screamed louder. "You seek to redress wrongs done to you and your kind for a millennium but this is not worthy of your magnificence! Your kind are all but gone yet you waste your wrath upon those who have done you no harm. You have shown your might and none will ever forget the awesome fury you have unleashed, but if you continue you will be destroyed by forces you cannot comprehend." Another gout of flame lanced at the wreckage. Ping wept but kept up his screamed plea. "Think, oh ruler of the heavens! This is folly! In the land of our births there are still two dragons, if I understand the math, and only you can free them to become a mighty nation once again!" The dragon slowed its momentum and seemed to hang there in the air contemplating the words of the frightened gadfly, Chin Song Ping. Slowly the immense form pivoted in a sky filled with billowing black smoke and gouts of crimson, both from the conflagration below and the angry sky overhead. Majestically, the thing oriented itself toward the ocean stretching endlessly to the west. Ping almost lost his hold as he slumped back in relief.

First he thought how much he enjoyed being a hero but decided that he shouldn't overdo such behavior as others might come to expect it of him. Then his thoughts became more practical. He was flying on a dragon out toward open water and below lay only ruin, leading to that savage sea. His planning, he decided, might have been a bit more foresighted.

Suddenly a small hail of large metal pellets scorched the air above his head sending several feathers flying. He looked up and heard a loud buzz as a fragile canvas and wood craft slowly descended from the cloud above. "Damn it man, how can I get off a decent shot if you keep waggling these wings back and forth like an epileptic goose?" a voice boomed as a huge iron rifle barrel slipped over the side of the craft.

Ping was never one much for social niceties but he understood well enough that one should never ignore a presidential invitation. He sprang with all his might at the wheel axel that was right over his head, shouting in what was left of his ragged voice. "Mr. President Teddy Roosevelt, sir, DO NOT SHOOT!"

☯

In the following days, volumes were written about the great 1906 San Francisco earthquake, but no mention was ever made of dragons or presidents. The Secret Service was good for something after all. The power of the Tongs and the influence of the Chinese Benevolent Society was broken with the destruction of Chinatown, which was eventually rebuilt in a manner more understandable to the western mind.

Roosevelt's reforms against tainted meat were enacted as the law of the land. Thousand-year-old Chinese dragon meat was not the only cause worth his ardor, it seemed, and Roosevelt was off to champion something else before the ink was dry on the bill. Without the monies from the sale of dragons as foodstuffs, the Emperor Guangxu failed in his coup to wrest power back from the Empress Dowager Cixi. The Quing Dynasty died five years later leaving China to almost half a century of civil wars and ultimately the rise of Communism.

☯

"I do." Ping said breathlessly and kissed his beautiful bride. They were a picture of splendor, he in a white silk suit and she in a frothy creation of whites and lavenders hastily erected by an army of the finest seamstresses in Washington DC. Her smile was dazzling against her rich coffee-brown skin and her beauty hadn't diminished in the slightest since he had first laid eyes on her across a garishly lit cave twenty-five years earlier.

"Well," She laughed as she threw her hands around his neck, "Everything's still here, so it looks like we saved the world again! And this time was so much easier."

Perhaps Ping would finally find time to share the details of his dress-finding excursion tonight, in their honeymoon bed.

Abruptly, five laughing children, aged fifteen and down, engulfed them in a weave of arms and legs. Fireworks went off overhead lighting up the cherry blossoms that fell all about.

Ping still couldn't recall for sure if he had voted for Roosevelt in the previous election but vowed to vote twice for him the next time he ran.

"Perfect story to end with, kid." The first rays of light were streaming through the cracks between the boards that covered the lone window.

Everyone gave a quiet clap as Tommy bowed his head to receive the appreciation. "Thanks for giving me a chance to hear them once again, for myself. They have never grown old for me."

Suddenly someone screamed outside and the staccato sounds of machine guns and rifles brought the war back into focus in an instant. Without hesitation or discussion, Fred and Tommy pushed their charges to the ground and crouched with teeth bared at the door. Whatever was going to happen next, these men were in their care and they would defend them to the last.

But the screaming and shooting continued for several more minutes. When it died down, all they heard was the terrible sound of a blade hacking into meat. Then, all of a sudden, a head poked through the door. The door had not opened but there was the head anyway.

A cheerful voice greeted them. "Hello! I am looking for Tommy Chin—oh, there you are."

"Grandfather Ping?" He would have fainted but he still had a responsibility to the men who were now making their way to their feet again.

Only Corporal Tragger spoke up as he could not see the apparition which had now entered the room fully. "What is it? What the Hell is going on?!"

The spirit bowed to them. "I am Chin Song Ping, most honored grandfather of the young scamp who stands with you. It is most peculiar that you can see me at all but I suppose that is because you were all so recently close to death yourselves."

Tommy stuttered. "W-w-w-hat the…"

Ping looked puzzled. "Did you not send a message to your grandmother? She woke us both out of a sound sleep and insisted that we help you immediately. I trust that your grandmother did not poison me for nothing.

The sergeant found his voice. "P-p-p-oison?"

"It was all we could come up with on short notice. She mixed up a fast-acting potion and I was dead almost immediately. Unpleasant, but it did produce the desired results. Once I was quite dead, Death showed up to claim my soul or whatever this is." He plucked at his translucent nightshirt. "I knew that with a war on he was probably on a tight schedule. Well, I simply refused to accompany him till he gave me my change from our last encounter."

Tommy, and indeed all the men, stared at him with puzzled disbelief.

"Oh, come now, I have told you of my trip into the afterlife when last I was in New Orleans. To make a long story somewhat shorter, we argued the point till he agreed to do me one small favor."

Duke raised his hand like a befuddled schoolboy. Ping smiled at him and granted him leave to speak. "What one small favor?"

"Ah yes, in lieu of gold I had him check to see if Tommy was scheduled to die tonight. He was and along with him you fine American boys. He agreed that in the midst of a war that it wasn't important which six men died—just that he filled his quota." Ping frowned and tilted his wrinkled head. "Sadly, there are now German mothers who will never see their sons again as Death has slaughtered them all, and is now escorting their souls to Valhalla or wherever valiant German warriors go these days."

"No shit?" Russ whispered.

"No excrement at all, I assure you. Louise has turned my empty body into a zombie so that it will not stiffen up till I can return to it."

A dark, gray shape congealed in the air behind Ping. In its hand was a farmer's scythe still dripping blood. "Does this balance the scales between us Chin Song Ping?" the voice was like thunder with a chest cold.

Tommy raced forward. "Oh, Grandfather don't you understand? You are dead now. I never wanted you to die instead of me," he wailed.

Ping gestured furtively at the cards from the uncompleted game of solitaire still spread out on the ground and they flew to his hand. He tucked them away without comment. "Dead. Yes, I suppose so and what a tragedy to be cut down in my prime. Still, perhaps I shall think of something." He winked and turned to his dark companion. "Yes, scales balanced—books balanced—and were I not wearing only a night shirt I would balance myself upon my head. Lead on, o' most dreaded one." As they vanished Tommy was sure he heard the soft shuffle of the deck of cards.

☯

Ten minutes later, a group of American GI's arrived with a tank leading the way. None of the men who awaited them; Cole, Tragger, Chin, Freeman, Duke or Winston, ever even tried to explain the mutilated, dead German soldiers. They pleaded shell-shock and one look into their eyes quashed all argument. Later that year, the Germans surrendered and the war in Europe was over.

Tommy continued to tell stories of his grandfather and in turn those stories were passed on by the generations that followed him. Death certificates were never issued for either Ping or Louise but then love never really dies—nor do stories.

## THE END OF
## CHIN SONG PING AND THE LONG, LONG NIGHT

# Acknowledgements

*The Venerable Travels of Ling Fung* is based on characters in "The Venerable Assassin" in *Under a Dark Sign*, edited by Rebecca McFarland Kyle and J.A. Campbell, published by Wolfsinger Publications and on characters in *The Two Devils* and *The Devil's Due*, originally published by LBF Books.

"Chin Song Ping and the Fists of Steel" first appeared in *Penny Dread Tales* Vol. 1 published by Rune Wright Publishing

"Chin Song Ping and the Fifty-Three Thieves" first appeared in *Six-Guns Straight From Hell* published by Science Fiction Trails Publishing.

"Chin Song Ping and the Hungry Ghosts" first appeared in *Gunslingers and Ghost Stories* published by Science Fiction Trails Publishing.

"Chin Song Ping and the Dragon Merchants" first appeared in *Tales of the Talisman*, volume 7, issue 4 published by Hadrosaur Productions.

# About the Authors

**Laura Givens** is a Jill of all trades, creatively speaking. She has had many short stories published but *Chin Song Ping and the Long, Long Night* is the closest she has come to a lengthier tome. She also contributed the cover here and is best known for her book and magazine covers in many genres and for numerous publishers. She took a side trip into producing coloring books last year and has recently been fiddling around with "found art" sculpture. She has written and produced screenplays, been a production silk screener and trod the boards doing comedy improv. She often wonders what she wants to be when she grows up.

**David B. Riley** has written six novels and more than 100 short stories which have appeared in magazines and anthologies around the world. He writes horror and science fiction and is an active member of the Horror Writers Association (HWA) David is also editor of 15 horror, science fiction and weird western anthologies and both edits and is the art director of the annual *Science Fiction Trails* Magazine and its predecessor, *Trails: Intriguing Stories of the Old West*. David currently lives in Tucson, Arizona.

www.ingramcontent.com/pod-product-compliance
Lightning Source LLC
Chambersburg PA
CBHW020118180626
46812CB00006B/2654